HERE
THE
WHOLE
TIME

HERE THE WHOLE TIME

VITOR MARTINS

TRANSLATED BY LARISSA HELENA

PUSH

Originally published in Brazilian Portuguese in 2017 as *Quinze Dias* by Globo Alt.

Text copyright © 2017 by Vitor Martins

English translation © 2020 by Larissa Helena

Library of Congress Cataloging-in-Publication Data

Names: Martins, Vitor, 1991– author. | Helena, Larissa, translator.
Title: Here the whole time / Vitor Martins; translated by Larissa Helena.
Other titles: Quinze dias. English
Description: First edition. | New York, NY: PUSH, 2020. | "Originally
    published in Brazilian Portuguese in 2017 as Quinze Dias by Globo
    Alt." | Audience: Ages 14–up. | Audience: Grades 10–12. |
    Summary: When Felipe, who is very insecure about his weight, is
    forced to spend winter break with his long-term crush, Caio, he
    must face his unresolved issues head-on.
Identifiers: LCCN 2020022252 (print) | LCCN 2020022253 (ebook) |
    ISBN 9781338620825 (hardcover) | ISBN 9781338675948 (ebook)
Subjects: CYAC: Overweight persons—Fiction. | Self-esteem—Fiction. |
    Gays—Fiction. | Mothers and sons—Fiction. | Single-parent
    families—Fiction. | Brazil—Fiction.
Classification: LCC PZ7.1.M3742 Her 2020 (print) |
    LCC PZ7.1.M3742 (ebook) | DDC [Fic]—dc23
LC record available at https://lccn.loc.gov/2020022252
LC ebook record available at https://lccn.loc.gov/2020022253

1 2020

Printed in the U.S.A.   23
First edition, November 2020
Book design by Baily Crawford

FOR ANYONE WHO HAS EVER GOTTEN
INTO A POOL WITH THEIR SHIRT ON

BEFORE

I AM FAT.

I'm not "chubby" or "husky" or "big boned." I'm heavy, I take up space, and people look at me funny on the street. I know there are plenty of people in this world who have much greater problems than I do here in Brazil, but I can't think about other people's suffering when I have my own issues to deal with at school. High school has been my own personal hell for the last two and a half years.

Sometimes I feel like the list of nicknames for fat people is endless. That isn't to say that this list is especially *creative*, but I'm always impressed with the sheer number of nicknames that guys at school come up with, when it would be so much easier to just call me Felipe.

Ever since I broke a chair in geography class at the beginning of the school year, people have sung "Wrecking Ball" whenever I pass by them in the halls. Two weeks after, another kid in my class broke his chair, but no one sings a Miley Cyrus song at him. You guessed it—he's skinny.

I've always been fat, and living in this body for seventeen years has made me an expert at ignoring comments from others. Which isn't to say that I'm used to it. It's hard to get used to it with daily reminders that you're a piece of demolition equipment. I've just gotten used to pretending that they're not talking about me.

Last year, without telling anyone, I bought one of those teen magazines that come with boy band posters inside. I like boy bands (more than I have the courage to admit), but what made me buy it was a burst on the cover that said, "Insecure about your body? Get over it, girl!"

According to the magazine, an overweight teenager who wants to be cool and have friends has to make up for their weight somehow. Basically, if you're really funny, or super stylish, or very likable, no one will notice that you're fat. I thought for a moment about how I compensated for it. I couldn't come up with anything.

I mean, I consider myself a funny guy. People love me online (543 Twitter followers and counting). But when I try to socialize in real life, I'm a big loser. I totally fail the likability test. And my style? Ha-ha. I'd define it as sneakers, jeans, and a reasonably clean gray T-shirt. It's hard to have cool clothes when you're a size XXL.

I flipped through the rest of the magazine, took the "Which celebrity would be your BFF?" quiz (I got Taylor

Swift), and then threw it out. I didn't want to be reminded that I have nothing to offer.

But today everything will be different. It's the last day of school before winter break—the day I've been looking forward to since the school year started. Winter break lasts twenty-two days. Twenty-two glorious days free of fat jokes, nicknames, and ugly looks.

I jump out of bed early to make sure I'm on time for school, and when I get to the kitchen, my mom is already up, painting a canvas. Three years ago, my mom quit her job at an accounting firm to become an artist. And it's been three years since our kitchen last resembled a normal one, because there are canvases, paint, and clay everywhere.

"Good morning, my angel," she says with a smile that should be impossible for someone who's been awake since seven a.m.

My mom is gorgeous. For real. She has big, animated eyes; her full hair is always tied up; and she's slim. Which means that before he walked out on us when he found out my mom was pregnant with me, my father made it a point to leave me with the fat gene. Thanks a lot, Dad.

"Good morning. You have paint on your chin. But you look beautiful, anyway," I say hurriedly as I grab a cheese sandwich and look for my keys.

"Felipe, I'm not sure if I told you, but this afternoon—"

"Sorry, can't talk—already late! See you later, love you, bye!" I answer, closing the door behind me.

To be honest, I'm never running late, but my anxiety makes me believe that the sooner I get to school, the sooner I can get it over with. Which, unfortunately, makes absolutely no sense.

I press the elevator button three times more than I have to as I finish my sandwich. And when the door opens, there he is. Caio, my neighbor from apartment 57. I swallow the dry piece of bread that's still in my mouth, rub my hand over my chin to make sure there are no crumbs left on my face, then step inside.

I whisper a "Good morning" so low that even I can't hear it. He doesn't respond. He's wearing earbuds and focusing on a book. I wonder if he's really listening to music while reading, or if he's the kind of guy who puts earbuds in so he won't be bothered. If option two is the right answer, I can't say I blame Caio from apartment 57. Because I always do that, too.

The elevator takes about forty seconds to go from the third floor, where I live, to the ground floor, but it feels like forty years have passed by the time the doors open again. I just stand there, not knowing what to do, and Caio walks out without even noticing that I was there. I wait three minutes in the hallway before leaving the building.

The last day of classes drags by. I only have to turn in a history paper and take a philosophy exam. And when I finish the test before everyone else, I'm desperate to get out of there.

"Already done, Butterball?" I hear someone say as I get up awkwardly from my tiny desk.

Mrs. Gomes, the teacher, collects my answer sheet and says, "Have a great vacation, Felipe," looking deep into my eyes. It feels like a look of compassion that says, "I know you can't take the other students' picking on you anymore, but stand your ground. You're strong. And there's absolutely nothing wrong with being fat. I know it's inappropriate to say this because I'm your teacher and I'm fifty-six years old, but you're quite the catch."

Or maybe I'm not that good at interpreting sympathetic looks and she really is just wishing me a great vacation after all.

When I get to the hallway, I see some girls saying goodbye to each other and (believe it or not) crying. As if winter break didn't last only twenty-two days. As if we didn't live in a small town where all you have to do is poke your head out a window to see half the school right there on the sidewalk. As if the internet didn't exist.

If my life were a musical, now would be the moment when I'd cross the school gates, singing a song about freedom, and people in the streets would dance in a tightly synchronized choreography behind me. But my life is not a musical, and when I walk through the gate, I hear someone yell, "Butterbaaaall!" I just lower my head and keep walking.

✳

My apartment building is close to school. It's only a fifteen-minute walk, and I like to do it every day so I'll have something to say when my doctor asks if I exercise regularly.

The only problem is all the sweating. After my obvious self-esteem issues and my absolutely lovely classmates, I think sweat is the thing I hate the most in life.

By the time I get home, I'm melting like a wax figure. My mom is in the same spot as when I left her. Except now she has a lot more paint stains on her clothes, and her painting is almost done. Today she painted a lot of blue circles (she's been in a blue phase for the past few months) that, if you look at them from just the right angle, appear to be two dolphins kissing. I think.

Besides the usual mess, there are pans on the stove, and the apartment smells like lunch. Actual lunch, not yakisoba leftovers from last night's takeout. The idea of starting the break with a proper lunch excites me.

"Hello, boys. How was school?" she asks, without lifting her eyes from the painting.

"Last time I checked, you only have one son, Mom."

"Ah, I thought you'd come home together. You and Caio, from 57." She turns around and gives me a kiss on the forehead.

I'm confused, but my mom doesn't seem to notice, because she doesn't add anything else. I go to my room to put down my backpack, and I'm startled when I realize it's been cleaned. My mom changed the sheets, organized my shelf, and picked up the crumpled socks from under the bed.

"Mom! What did you do to my room? Where are my socks?!" I shout.

"In the drawer! Imagine how embarrassing it would be if the neighbors' son came into your room to find eleven pairs of socks all over the place!" she yells back.

Eleven? Whoa. Impressive.

I go back to the kitchen so I won't have to scream. "What was that about the neighbors' son?"

"I told you, didn't I? He's coming today. He's staying with us for fifteen days. His parents are going to a conference on penguins. Or a second honeymoon. Who knows. Anyway, Sandra asked me to keep an eye on Caio while they're away. I was a little surprised because he's old enough to stay by himself, no? But it's not a big deal, and he's a good kid."

The more my mom talks, the more shocked I become.

"You didn't tell me! I can't have a houseguest right now, not during winter break—and for fifteen days! I have *plans*!"

"Internet and bingeing Netflix?" She rolls her eyes. "Really big plans you have, Felipe."

She knows me well.

"But . . . but . . . doesn't he have any relatives? Can't he stay by himself? You and his mom aren't even friends! What kind of a person doesn't trust her own teenage son to stay home alone but trusts a complete stranger?"

"Well, no, we're not exactly *friends*-friends. We chat in the hallway sometimes. She always holds the elevator door for me. And we used to talk a lot when you and Caio played in the pool when you were younger. Good times, those. But that's beside the point. Help me organize the kitchen and set the table. He'll be here any minute!"

I just stand there in disbelief. My face is sweaty, terrified, immobile. Like a painting my mom would make on a bad day.

You're probably thinking, *Calm down, dude, it's just the neighbor kid!* Maybe it's time I told you about Caio, the neighbor kid from apartment 57.

※

Our apartment complex has a large recreation area with a tennis court that no one ever uses (because, honestly, who plays tennis?), a little playground that's falling apart, and a pool that's neither big nor small but is always crowded on hot days.

When I was a kid, that pool was my very own private

ocean. I spent hours swimming from one end to the other and re-creating scenes from *The Little Mermaid*. And it was in that pool that I met Caio. I can't quite recall the day, or how we started talking. We were pool buddies, and I can't remember what my childhood was like before that.

If you're a fat eight-year-old boy, no one calls you Butterball. Everyone thinks you're cute, pinches your cheeks, and always makes it very clear how much they want to eat you up. In a sweet way. Weird, but still sweet.

When I was eight, I didn't feel embarrassed about running around wearing nothing but a Speedo, or jumping into the pool and splashing water everywhere. Because when you're eight, it's okay. And that's how Caio and I became friends. We never went to the same school (Caio goes to a private school on the other side of town). But when we were younger and it was a hot day, I knew all I had to do was go downstairs to the pool, and Caio would be there, ready to swim with me. Rainy days were the worst.

We never talked. Kids don't really talk when they're at the pool. We would scream and dive and compete to see who could stay underwater the longest. We didn't have time to talk because, at any moment, Caio's mom could stick her head out the window, yelling his name, and the fun would be over just like that. His mom was always that type. The type who yells.

9

Somewhere in the middle of all the fun and no talking, I had a day I've never forgotten. I must have been around eleven, and after almost an entire afternoon playing sharks and pirates (I was the pirate, Caio the shark), I suggested without an ounce of fear, "Do you wanna play mermaids?"

None of the other kids in the building knew that I loved to play mermaids. It was something I did just for me. I was afraid of what the other boys might think of me if they found out that when I went underwater, in my head I was Ariel. And that deep at the bottom of the pool, I kept my imaginary collection of forks, mirrors, and thingamabobs.

Caio just smiled, crossed his legs to form a tail, and dove underwater. He didn't care to know how to play. He didn't say he'd play only if he could be a mer*man*. He merely went along with my silly fantasy and we swam like mermaids until dusk. It was the best day ever.

After that, everything went by in a blur. As I grew up, the shame of wearing a Speedo in front of Caio grew with me. I didn't quite understand what I felt, exactly, but I know that when I was twelve, I started wearing a shirt whenever I went to the pool. And after I turned thirteen, I never set foot in the pool again.

At thirteen my body began to change, hair started grow-ing everywhere, and I had this urge to kiss someone on the lips. And I wanted that first person to be Caio.

It was ridiculous how hard I had fallen for Caio. But he's way out of my league. It's like being in love with the lead singer of your favorite boy band: All you can do is watch from afar and dream.

Now do you understand my despair? Fat, gay, and in love with a boy who won't even acknowledge my *Good morning* in the elevator. Everything could go wrong. Everything *will* go wrong. And I don't even have time to come up with an exit strategy, because the doorbell is ringing. And my mom is opening the door. And I, of course, am covered in sweat.

So it begins.

DAY 1

"COME IN, COME IN!" my mom says, pulling Caio inside while fixing his bangs.

Boundaries, Mom. Boundaries.

I was expecting him to arrive with his mom and a laundry list of instructions. But here he is, all by himself.

"My parents got on the first flight to Chile this morning," he explains to my mom.

The two must get about two minutes of conversation in while I'm just standing here, watching. Doing all I can to sweat less and act normal.

"Help him with the suitcase, son!" my mom says, snapping her fingers in front of my face and bringing me back to reality.

A reality in which I'm wheeling a huge leopard-print suitcase full of clothes that belong to my hot neighbor—who, by the way, is spending the next fifteen days with me—into my room. I take a deep breath and put the suitcase in a corner, between the closet and my desk. Then another deep breath, just to be on the safe side.

"Sorry about the giant suitcase. That was all my mom,"

Caio says, appearing out of nowhere in my bedroom door and scaring me a little, which I try to hide with a tight smile.

I don't say anything, because I don't know what to say. I want to show that I'm funny, but out of the three jokes that I can come up with, two require knowledge of specific episodes of *Friends*, and the other, I'm almost sure, would be offensive to Caio's mother.

"Boys! Lunchtime!" my mother shouts, rescuing me from the embarrassing situation.

"I'm going to take a quick shower and then I'll be right there!" I yell back, running to the bathroom and leaving Caio behind.

When I step into the shower, I'm finally able to breathe. The water relaxes me, and I can think about the situation more calmly. I know how to talk to people, I'm kind, I'm pleasant (maybe). He's just a guest.

It's like when my great-aunt Lourdes comes to visit every year on All Souls' Day. Her husband is buried here in town, and when she comes to visit his grave, she always spends the whole week with us. Great-Aunt Lourdes cooks everything with green peppers and uses her spit to fix my eyebrows. Caio won't be doing any of that (I hope), so this should be even easier.

When I get out of the shower, I feel calmer and more confident that everything is going to be fine. It was just another one of the thousands of times in my life when I was being overdramatic for nothing. I should be used to it by now. I can almost laugh at myself, but the laughter doesn't come. Because I suddenly realize that I didn't bring any clean clothes to the bathroom. All I have with me is a towel and a pile of sweaty clothes.

I need to think fast, because I don't want Caio to think I'm taking too long in the shower. You know what they say about boys who take too long in the shower. Well, there you go.

I press my ear against the door and hear voices in the kitchen. My mom is there and Caio must be eating his lunch. I think I can go down the hallway really fast and get to my room without being seen. I wrap a towel around me, play the *Mission: Impossible* theme song in my head, and take three long strides to my bedroom.

And when I open the door . . .

I.

Want.

To.

Die.

Caio is sitting there with a book in his hands. He looks at me, startled, and tries to say something, but I speak first. Yell, actually.

"GET OUT OF MY ROOM! NOW!"

Frightened, he gets up and leaves. I slam the door, lock it, and immediately start to cry. It's not a loud and dramatic cry, the kind where you lean your back against the wall and slide down to the floor. It's just a single tear, running down my face, and I can't help but feel ashamed. Ashamed because I'm all wet, naked under a *Star Wars* towel that doesn't even fit around my whole waist. Ashamed because Caio saw me like this. And I screamed at him. And this is only day one.

I hear the doorknob turn, but the door is locked.

"Felipe, is everything okay? What happened? Come have lunch!" my mom says on the other side of the door.

By the tone in her voice, I can't tell if she's worried about or mad at me. Maybe both.

"I'll eat later. I'm not hungry," I lie.

I open the closet to get dressed and start my usual ritual. For a few seconds, I look in the mirror, naked, and take stock of every single detail that bothers me about myself. Some days I like to notice the small things, like a new zit or a red stretch mark running up the side of my stomach. Other days, I prefer to analyze my whole body, looking from side to side and wondering what it would be like if I were thin.

But today I don't waste too much time in front of the mirror. Even though I'm locked in here, having Caio in my house makes me feel more exposed than ever. I put on a random T-shirt, which falls uncomfortably around my still-wet body, and a pair of shorts.

My pride keeps me from leaving the bedroom. I lie in bed, eat half a sleeve of cookies that I found in my backpack, and kill time on my phone. I don't want to be alone. I want my mom to come talk to me. I want her to give me advice and a plate of food because, honestly, half a pack of cookies? Who am I kidding? I need a real lunch!

But my mom doesn't come.

Two hours go by, and I finally decide to tiptoe stealthily into the kitchen. My mom is painting a new canvas, and the apartment is silent.

"There's a plate for you in the microwave," she says as soon as she sees me coming. I can tell she's annoyed.

I try to mutter a thank-you, but she only lets out a long sigh—the kind that comes right before a lecture.

"Felipe, my son, I'm not stupid. I am your mother. I know you well and I know why you yelled at Caio," she says softly, probably because Caio is in the living room. "But you've never raised your voice to anyone, and you're not about to start now. I know you like peace and quiet, and to be left alone. I understand all of that. But this is just for fifteen days, and I need your help. You're not a child any-more. I'm not going to take you by the hand and make you apologize to your friend. But you will finish eating, put a smile on your face, go into the living room, and apologize to Caio."

I roll my eyes.

"And just for that, you've earned the privilege of doing the dishes afterward," she concludes with a satisfied smile.

✳

I'm standing in the middle of the living room, hoping a meteorite will hit me and put an end to all this awkwardness. Or that a black hole will open up beneath my feet and swallow me whole. I'm not picky.

Caio is sitting on the couch, reading the same book he had with him this morning in the elevator (*The Fellowship of the Ring* by Tolkien—one of my favorites, by the way). Everything seems so out of place. It's a little surreal to see him sitting on our old, floral-patterned couch, surrounded by all my mom's unfinished paintings and a framed photo of a ten-year-old me wearing an indigenous outfit for a school play—which, besides being super embarrassing, is also pretty offensive.

He sticks out like a sore thumb in the middle of all the mess, like an alien in the center of a Renaissance painting (and this is probably the worst comparison you're going to read today).

He's definitely noticed me standing here. It's kind of hard not to notice someone my size. But even so, he doesn't look at me. He's concentrating on the book, his bangs falling slightly over his left eye. It makes me want to lick his face.

I wish I could sit next to him and see where he is in the book. Ask what he thinks about the story so far. I want to know if he's the type who watches the movie and then reads the book, or the other way around.

I clear my throat, exaggerating the volume a little so he'll realize I have something to say.

"I'm sorry I yelled at you," I say.

He looks up at me, deep into my eyes, and I can't tell if he's mad or feels sorry for me. I don't like either option.

"It's okay," he says dryly.

Caio lowers his head and continues to read.

Wow, what a conversation. Nice work, Felipe.

*

Dinner is even weirder. We eat in the living room, watching a rerun of a reality show about wedding dresses. Me, my mom, and Caio squeeze onto our tiny couch, eyes glued to a bride who's panicking because the wedding is three days away and the dress won't zip all the way. I could never lose enough weight in three days to fit into a dress, so I eat my dinner sending positive vibes to the bride on TV.

My mom forces small talk with Caio, and it's almost insufferable how nice he is about it. They chat about a prime-time soap opera that my mom doesn't even watch, and yet she knows everything that's going to happen in the next episode. Caio compliments her food, and despite the fact that it's the same rice, beans, beef, and french fries from lunch, the compliment sounds sincere.

"For real, Rita! Your food tastes amazing. My mom is so neurotic about what we eat at home. I already told my dad she's taking it too far. She won't even put salt in our food," Caio says between bites.

"Don't even *think* about telling Sandra that you ate fries here! She'd never let you come back," my mom says, giggling.

And while the two of them talk as if they are best friends, I'm on the other end of the couch listening. Just listening and never speaking.

I know this will sound ridiculous, but I'm kind of jealous. Jealous of Caio, because my mom is only focused on him and paying no attention to me. And to make matters worse, I'm jealous of my mom. Caio barely got here and he's already praising her cooking. I'm jealous because I wish he would talk to me. About food, about his mom, about soap operas— about anything at all.

When the TV show about wedding dresses ends (the bride loses the weight, the dress is gorgeous, everyone cries, *fin*), my mom gives me a light tap on the shoulder, and I know it means the dishes are my responsibility. Looks like she's not done punishing me for today's events.

While I organize the kitchen, my mom says good night to Caio (all smiles, of course), and I do my best not to freak out when I realize that in a few hours he and I will be sleeping in the same bedroom. Inches away from each other.

Our apartment is small, and we've never had a guest room. But my bed is one of those that you can pull a handle and *ta-da!* there's another mattress hidden underneath. My mom chose this one thinking of all the friends I might invite for a sleepover. I can't remember the last time the extra bed was used by anyone other than my great-aunt Lourdes.

Sharing a room with Caio for fifteen days could result in an unlimited series of disasters. In the time it takes me to wash three plates, I am able to come up with a list of fifty-four disasters that I might cause just by sleeping in the same bedroom as him. The majority of the list is pretty gross (hello, night farts), but some are natural and inevitable (like morning wood).

Jumping to the worst-case scenario is my specialty. But I decide to stop thinking this way when I come up with a hypothetical situation in which I'm a sleepwalker (for the record, I'm not) and I attack Caio in the middle of the night. Which . . . would be awkward.

I wash the dishes, dry them, dry them again, and then put everything away inside the cabinets. I try to waste as much time as I can so I won't have to face bedtime. I wipe the sweat off my forehead with a dish towel (sorry, Mom) and go back into the living room.

I don't know how long it took me to wash everything, but it was long enough for Caio to put on his pajamas, find a pillow, and lie down on the couch with a book, his feet on a folded blanket. For a split second, I don't know what to say. Not that I was planning to say anything, but even still, I don't react. I try to rationalize the following information in my head:

- Caio is probably going to sleep in the living room.

- Because he has a pillow and a blanket with him. In the living room.

- Caio is already in his pajamas.

- Is Caio going to sleep in the living room???

- Apparently, he is, as he's wearing his pajamas. In the living room.

- Wow. Caio in pajamas.

- I guess I won't have to worry about night farts and morning wood after all.

- And, yet, I don't want Caio to sleep in the living room.

- I want him to sleep next to me.

- Especially if he's wearing *those pajamas*.

I could go on for hours on the topic of Caio's pajamas. They're navy blue and white, with a maritime theme. The top is striped and has a deep V-neck. The bottoms have little anchors and boats. But I can't focus on the design because, where his shorts end, his legs begin. I could dedicate another two hours to the topic of Caio's legs. His thighs are thick and have some hair on them, and his tan skin is even shinier under the light of the chandelier in the living room. (Actually, the chandelier is a round paper lantern that my mom decided to make after watching a YouTube tutorial.)

If you look at him from just the right angle, Caio looks like Aladdin. And one second before I start imagining the two of us flying over a whole new world on a magic carpet ride, Caio clears his throat louder than he needs to and looks at me. I don't know how long I've been standing here, gawking at him and embarrassing myself over a pair of thighs.

"I'm sleeping in the living room," Caio says matter-of-factly, as if I needed to be Sherlock Holmes to deduce as much.

I think about insisting that he sleep in my bedroom. I think about telling him that the couch is too lumpy and will be murder on his back (which is true). But who am I kidding? Of course he won't agree. Not after seeing me naked, soaking wet, and wrapped in a towel, screaming, *GET OUT OF MY ROOM!*

I offer him some water, tea, an extra pillow, but he doesn't accept any of it. When Caio turns his attention back to his book, I realize it's better if I just go away. I walk into my room and slam the door gently enough so as not to wake my mom but loud enough to sound dramatic.

I decide to sleep in my pajamas tonight. I usually sleep in an old T-shirt and shorts. I pull the pajamas out of the drawer. They don't have a sexy sailor theme; they're beige, huge, and hideous. When I look at myself in the mirror, I look like a page straight out of the *Guinness Book of World Records*, showing the record holder for world's largest sugar cookie.

I'm such an embarrassment.

I fling myself onto the bed and watch cat videos online until I fall asleep.

DAY 2

TODAY IS A SATURDAY. I usually love Saturdays. I get to sleep in and watch three movies in a row, and my mom always bakes a cake. Every Saturday is like that, and the tradition has never been broken. I like traditions, especially ones that involve cake.

And yet I don't wake up excited today. I didn't sleep well and spent the whole night thinking about how much easier it would be if my life were *Freaky Friday.* My mom and I would swap bodies, and she'd have to deal with Caio. I'd just sit there and watch, smiling and painting. We'd stay in each other's bodies for fifteen days, and when Caio left, the spell would wear off.

I leave my absurd fantasies behind and decide to get out of bed. It's early, six in the morning. I look in the mirror and notice that I'm still inside my own body. Too bad. This story would be much better if I had magically switched bodies with my mom.

I walk out of the room to get a glass of water, and when I pass by the living room, there he is. Caio is asleep on the couch, and it's almost ridiculous how good-looking he is. I've never seen anyone who could look so beautiful even while sleeping. Not in real life, anyway. I've always thought the whole peaceful sleep thing, the thing where your chest moves up and down calmly in unison with your breathing, only happened in movies. In real life, people sleep with an elbow touching the back of their necks, one sock half-off, and drool streaking down their pillows.

Caio can't be real.

I think a whole seven minutes have passed, and here I stand, watching him sleep. Seven minutes. I need help. Seriously.

Water, Felipe! Water! I tell myself, trying to focus on the actual reason that got me out of the bedroom. I walk to the kitchen, trying not to make noise, but of course it all goes wrong, because I'm about as delicate as a mammoth. I open the closet without realizing my strength and two pans fall to the floor. In the morning quiet, it sounds more like two hundred.

I kneel down to clean the mess I just made and suddenly feel a presence in the kitchen. For a second I believe it might be the ghost of my dead grandma, who has decided now would be a good time to tell me the meaning of life or to give me advice about how to become emotionally stable. But of course it's not her (though I do miss you, Grandma!). It's Caio.

"Need help?" he asks, looking at me with the face of someone who's just been awoken by the clatter of two hundred pans crashing on the floor.

"No, no. It's okay!" I lie, because it's *not* okay. I'm crouching in my beige pajamas. And I am pretty sure my butt crack is showing. Big-time.

And those are all the words we exchange that morning. We go through a silent ritual where I pour a glass of water and offer it to him with a nod. He accepts it with a grunt that doesn't quite become an actual word. And we just stand there, drinking water, staring into nothingness without saying anything.

Caio stretches his back between sips (a lovely sight, I have to say) and I'm sure he woke up with a backache. It's impossible to sleep on our couch and wake up happy. Sleeping on a wet cardboard box would be more comfortable. I think about starting a conversation and asking if he slept okay, but I quickly give up. The silence is nearly unbearable now, and then he puts his glass in the sink and leaves.

I let out a sigh of relief.

*

The rest of the morning goes by slowly and torturously. After I woke him up, Caio didn't go back to sleep. He sits on the couch and picks up his book. I pace back and forth, trying to casually make it clear that I'm available. Totally not doing anything. Like 200 percent free as a bird. But he's so focused on his reading that I give up.

I go back to my room and watch YouTube tutorials for things I'll never make (today it's artisanal candles, ceramic bowls, and soaps). I can't quite explain it, but the time I spend on the internet somehow feels less like a waste when I'm learning something new.

Weekends always go by pretty quickly, but after lunch it feels like I've been living this same day for forty-five years. My mom is painting in the kitchen, and I find myself alone with Caio in the living room. It's cold outside, but of course I'm sweating. I'm sitting on the floor because it feels like the kind thing to do. Our floral couch was Caio's bed last night, and I don't want him to feel like I'm not respecting his space. My laptop is on my lap and I'm adding movies that I'll never watch to my watch list. Caio is still sitting on the couch, still reading *The Fellowship of the Ring*.

In the last few hours, I've come up with a theory. I believe Caio is already done with the book but he keeps rereading the final chapters over and over just so he won't have to talk to me. I know that sounds neurotic, but this time I'm *serious*. It just happened! I was debating whether it was worth adding *Legally Blonde 2* to my watch list (an easy call, because I absolutely love the first *Legally Blonde*, and bad sequels to good movies even more). I looked over at Caio quickly as I clicked "Add to List," and I caught him turning back a few pages in the book! He's rereading pages! All so he doesn't have to close the book and feel obligated to talk to me.

I'm officially the worst host in the world.

"It's cake day!" My mom walks into the living room, practically shouting with excitement. "But we're out of eggs and flour. I need butter, too, and I'm craving grapes." She's calling out the items as she writes them down one by one on a piece of paper. "Who wants to go to the supermarket for me?"

"I'll go!" Caio and I say at the same time.

"Great, you can go together!" my mom says with a smile, handing me the money and the grocery list.

*

The supermarket is two blocks from our building. It's a quick walk that I'm used to doing almost every day. But walking there with Caio by my side is a completely different experience. When I'm with him, people glance our way, and I don't know if they're reacting to how gorgeous he is or how fat I am. Or both.

I wonder what it would be like to walk down the street holding hands with someone. Just walking side by side, my fingers interlaced with Caio's while we bump into each other a little because I can't walk in a straight line to save my life. I think about how amazing it would be to walk into the store with his hand in mine, smiling at each other, as if we were Justin and Britney arriving at the American Music Awards in 2001, wearing denim from head to toe. The whole store looking at us and thinking we're the best couple of all time.

But that's never going to happen. Especially if we take into account the fact that we live in a town where no one would approve of two boys walking hand in hand in the grocery store. And the fact that Caio won't even *talk* to me.

"I think we should split the list," I say suddenly, without any context, because I have the social skills of a cheese grater.

"Huh?" Caio looks confused.

"The list. The items. We could divide and conquer, each one gets half the list. We'll meet at the checkout line and waste half the time!" I explain, my words all crashing into one another.

"Fine by me," Caio says with a crooked grin. His smile is a little awkward, but his teeth are perfect. He could star in one of those commercials with ripped models sitting by the pool, casually holding tubes of toothpaste.

I tear the shopping list in half, hand him a piece, and attempt to smile back. I say *attempt* only because most of the time when I smile, it looks like I'm having a stroke. I lower my head before he notices.

We walk into the store and head in different directions.

I check my half of the list, written in my mom's hurried handwriting:

- Eggs

- Grapes (the purple seedless kind)

- Milk (the cheapest brand)

Easy peasy. I go down the main aisle and grab a carton of milk. I can't find the purple grapes anywhere, so I decide to get the eggs. In my head, I'm in a competition with Caio to see who can find their three items first. At the end, there will be a finish line, with production assistants handing me a giant check as confetti falls from the sky.

I hurry to the egg aisle and suddenly feel the urge to turn around and run back home, because Jorge and Bruno are here. But they see me before I have a chance to escape.

A quick rundown on Jorge and Bruno: They go to the same school as me, and they're responsible for 80 percent of the nicknames that I've amassed over the last two years. Jorge was held back a couple of times, is almost nineteen years old, and has a full beard that would be cute if he wasn't such a jerk. Bruno is half my height; his hair is shaved on the sides, forming an undercut that didn't turn out quite right; and he could never be cute even if he were on an episode of *Queer Eye*.

They both start walking my way, and I pretend to concentrate on which eggs to buy. White or brown? Decisions, decisions . . .

"Well, if it isn't Butterball!" Bruno shouts, his high-pitched voice echoing across the aisle.

"Attention, shoppers: You'd better buy your food before the whale eats it all!" Jorge cups his hands around his mouth, as if he were announcing today's deals.

I try to pretend like nothing is happening, but that becomes much harder to do when Bruno starts poking me in the back, moving from one side to the other.

The two of them always split their work efficiently when it comes to tormenting me. Jorge prefers verbal offenses, while Bruno is the type who likes to get more handsy. I don't know which one I hate more.

"No use trying to hide," Jorge continues when he realizes I'm trying to remove myself from the situation. "You're so fat that not even the moon could cover all of you."

I roll my eyes, frustrated. As if this were the first time I've heard that one.

"You're so fat that . . . that . . ." Bruno starts to say, apparently not having thought of a punch line to his own joke.

Not knowing how to finish his sentence, he takes the easy route and, shoving me against the shelves behind me, catches me by surprise and twists my nipple—hard.

"Tittieeeees!" he says, almost in a whisper, in a sadistic tone of someone who's never had this much fun.

I try to defend myself by covering my chest, but I end up dropping the grocery basket I am holding, and when I bend down to pick it up, I'm almost certain I can hear Bruno calling me a fat ass. I'll never understand how someone half my size can manage to make me feel so small.

The two of them seem satisfied by the fun they've had at my expense and walk down the aisle as if nothing happened. I grab a carton of eggs at random, put it in the basket, and run out of there.

When Caio arrives with his three items, I'm desperate to get home.

"Can we leave now, please?!" I say, trying hard to sound calm and polite.

I pick the line that seems shortest and count each second that goes by. I'm so mad I feel like I'm about to explode. We get to the register, I pay for the groceries, and I walk out of the supermarket trying to forget what just happened.

I hurry back home, and Caio has no trouble keeping up with me. I need to get back as quickly as I can. I don't want to cry in front of him, but my eyes are already tearing up, and I'm so angry I can feel my face turn red. Caio must notice, because he asks if everything is all right, and I can tell he really means it when he asks.

"I couldn't find the grapes," I say, hoping this answer will satisfy him.

Caio doesn't say anything else.

*

When we get home, my mom is ready to start baking the cake. She seems a little frustrated when I throw the shopping bags on the table, come up with some excuse for not having found the grapes that she wanted, and announce that I'm going to my room.

It's funny how she can tell when I'm being dramatic and when I really need to be alone.

"I'll let you know when the cake is ready," she says, stroking my head. I leave her with Caio in the kitchen.

When I lock my bedroom door, the parts of my body that Bruno shoved into the shelves are still burning. I'm angry at him and Jorge for treating me the way they did. I'm angry at myself for letting it happen.

What happened at the supermarket wasn't anything new. This is my daily life. But at school I'm always ready, always alert. It's as if my school uniform came with a shield, because I know that when the last bell rings, I'll go home and be all right. When I went out to get groceries, I didn't have my shield. I wasn't ready, and they caught me by surprise.

I lie in bed and look at my comic book collection, wishing more than ever that I were a superhero. I'd take any superpower that would make me feel better. I want to create force fields so no one can touch me when I don't want to be touched. I want muscles of steel to break the noses of everyone who's ever hurt me. I want to be invisible so I can disappear and never come back.

Hours go by, and I don't even notice. I stare at the ceiling to try and distract myself. When I was a kid, the ceiling in my room was full of glow-in-the-dark stars. At some point in my teenage years, I thought I was too big to have stickers on the ceiling and ripped them all off, but today I regret it. I want my stars back. I'd have something to focus on if my glowing stickers were still up there.

My mind won't stop replaying the events at the super-market. Everything happened so fast, it couldn't have lasted even a full minute. But now I'm stuck in a never-ending loop of insults and roaring laughter. The laughter is the worst part. The sound of laughter can make you feel hopeless when the joke is on you.

The afternoon has already turned into evening when my mom knocks on my door. She tries to turn the knob, but I locked it.

"Son? Is everything all right?" she asks softly from the other side.

"I want to be alone, Mom."

"I baked a cake!" She tries to cheer me up.

Usually, those four words will do it. On a regular Saturday, it would be the best part of the day. Eating cake with my mom and watching any silly show on TV. It's usually enough to make me happy. But not today.

"I'll eat later." My voice is so low that I doubt she can hear it. But her footsteps fade away before I turn on the bed and try to fall asleep.

✳

I wake up a few hours later, starving. It's still dark out.

You know when you sleep outside your regular hours and wake up totally lost, not knowing what time it is, where you are, or what happened in the world in the meantime? Yeah, that.

I check the alarm clock; it's two a.m. I drag myself out of the bed, trying to decide if I'm more in need of food or a shower, and leave the bedroom. The apartment is silent and the hallway smells of cake. I walk to the kitchen and have a slice. (It was carrot cake, in case you were wondering.) I pass by the living room, and Caio is asleep on the couch. But he looks different. If he was sleeping all cute and peaceful last night, tonight he looks exhausted. His body is contorted, as if he were trying to get into an impossible yoga pose. Sleeping on that hard couch can't be good for anybody.

There's a comfortable guest bed in my room, and I wish I could pick Caio up and carry him to it. But I can't do that because A) I'm not strong enough to carry him, and B) I'm not out of my mind. Still, I try to help as much as I can. I close the curtains so the sunlight won't wake him up in the morning, and I fix his blanket, which was almost on the floor.

Before I head back to my room, I spot Caio's book on the coffee table. He spent the entire morning reading *The Fellowship of the Ring*, and the bookmark is still in the same spot, almost at the very end of the book. It's official. He's determined to reread the end of this book forever, just so he won't have to talk to me. And I can't let that happen.

I run to my bookshelf, grab my copy of *The Two Towers*, and place it right next to Caio's book. My book is way more beat-up than his. It's an old edition that my grandma gave to me, but I think it'll do the job. He might not want to talk to me, but he can at least know how the story continues.

I go back to my room in silence, and this time I leave the door open.

DAY 3

IT'S PAST NOON WHEN I wake up on Sunday. Two days into my vacation, and my sleep schedule is already screwed up. When I walk out of my bedroom, I realize the house is empty. Our apartment is pretty small, so it doesn't take me long to check all the rooms. No sign of my mom or Caio. While I look for my phone to call my mom, I think of possible reasons for why they've gone missing. My mind jumps to kidnapping, alien abduction, and zombie apocalypse.

The call goes straight to voice mail. She probably ran out of battery from playing *Candy Crush* before bed. I think of giving Caio a call, but I don't have his number. I get a little desperate as I ponder the best way to negotiate for my mom's life with kidnappers. Or, worse, to negotiate the future of the human race with aliens, who probably won't speak my language.

I keep pacing around the house, as if waiting for Caio and my mom to jump out from behind the curtains and yell, "SURPRISE!" at any point. My stomach starts to rumble, and I feel like a heartless monster for being hungry at a moment like this. Even so, I go to the kitchen to look for food and let out a sigh of relief when I find a note on the fridge.

Felipe,

I couldn't wake you up for the life of me! Going to the mall and taking Caio with me.

There's food for you in the microwave, just heat it up!

Love you!

And, right below, in handwriting I don't recognize, it says:

Thanks for the book. ;)

Four words and a little wink. At least it looks like a wink. I can't tell for sure because Caio's handwriting looks like chicken scratch (hey, nobody's perfect). Anyway, if it's between a wink or a really weird exclamation point, I'll go with option one. Caio left me four words and a little wink, and I can't stop smiling. I'm so excited, you'd think he stroked my hair and gave me a coupon for one kiss. But no, it's only four words. And a wink.

The wink is a good sign, right? It's a flirty smiley. Does this mean he's forgiven me? That he's thankful for the book and wants to give me a shot? The possibility makes me so happy that I almost forget to eat.

I shake my head to wake up from this dream in which Caio *flirts* with me, then reheat the food my mom left me. I have lunch in silence, watching the minutes go by on the microwave clock. It's two and a half hours slow. My mom and I keep forgetting to fix it.

It looks like I have the whole day to myself now but no idea what to do with it. I could use the alone time to work on some personal projects, but I'm the worst person in the universe when it comes to completing them.

I once tried writing a comic book that's set in my school. An explosion in a fictional lab (because my school isn't the kind that has a lab) gave my teachers superpowers. My favorites were the heroes, naturally, and the ones I hated were the villains. I wrote and illustrated two stories but gave up on the idea because A) I can't draw, and B) I could never get this thing published due to the extremely offensive content against my gym teacher.

After I realized how bad I was at drawing, I focused my angst into short stories. Some were actually kind of cool, and I thought it would be a good idea to put them out in the world. I created a blog and published my stories, but no one ever read them. I abandoned that project, too.

There was the time when I decided to learn how to play the guitar. My mom approved of the idea, even bought a guitar for me, and I started taking classes with Mr. Luiz, a retiree in our neighborhood who gives music lessons. I spent two months learning (trying to learn, really), but I knew in the first week that it wasn't going to work out. I had the willpower, and I even enjoyed practicing at home, but the truth is that I have no sense of rhythm. I can't play the guitar, can't clap my hands, can't even whistle.

Origami, cooking, juggling, belly dancing. I'm not good at anything! Maybe that's why I watch so many useless internet tutorials. I think I am, subconsciously, looking for something I might be good at, but I've never lucked out in the talent lottery.

I finish lunch without the slightest idea of what I'm going to do for the next few hours, but I feel determined and optimistic. So I decide to begin the afternoon by adjusting the microwave clock, taking my first step toward change.

*

In an ideal world, I'd have spent the entire afternoon composing a song, writing a poem, painting the next *Mona Lisa*. Caio would get home to find me focused on my work of art, and he'd find himself in awe and in love at the same time.

Of course, that's not what happens. I spent the entire afternoon catching up on my favorite TV shows, and when Caio and my mom open the door, it's already dark out. I sit up on the couch, startled, pull my T-shirt down to hide my belly button, and hug a pillow to camouflage the folds of my stomach, which appear when I sit down.

My mom is yapping away, and I feel sorry for Caio, for having to withstand her chatter all day long. The only thing my mom needs is a pair of willing ears, and she can talk for an eternity.

But when I look at Caio, I don't find a desperate plea for help in his eyes. He's smiling and looks happy. Actually, this is the happiest I've seen him since he came to stay with us.

"We went shopping!" my mom says, all excitement, walking down an imaginary catwalk while holding a bunch of bags from different shops. I can't contain a smile, because seeing my mom jokingly parading down the room makes me think that she could have been the prettiest model in the whole world.

"This morning I tried to wake you up in every possible way, but you were passed out." She keeps talking while she removes items from their bags, one by one. "So I grabbed Caio and said, 'Let's go to the mall!' Because this boy has been stuck in this apartment since Friday. Imagine if the police found out! They'd lock me up and throw away the key!" She starts laughing at her own joke.

Caio laughs, too.

"Of course, I bought a thing or two for you so you wouldn't be jealous, now that I have a second son!" my mom says while rummaging through the bags for my presents. "Here!" she yells in excitement, and hands me a bag.

"Thanks, Mom," I say, a bit uncertain, because that's what Caio's presence does to me.

I stick my hand in the bag and feel like dying when the first thing I pull out is a pack of underwear.

"I got you new briefs," my mom starts, "because I went to wash one of yours, and for god's sake, Felip—"

"THANKS, MOM!" I repeat, almost shouting in order to get her to stop talking. Caio muffles a laugh.

I hide the briefs under the couch pillow and go back to exploring the clothes in the bag. One gray shirt, one black sweatshirt, one pair of jeans, as if I were the most boring participant in the history of a fashion TV show. But the last item surprises me. At first I think it's a tablecloth, but it's a checkered flannel shirt. It's black and red, kind of like a lumberjack Kurt Cobain. It looks nice, but it's not my style.

"Caio picked that one! I wanted to get you something a little more dressy. But Caio liked the color," my mom explains, and I don't know how to react.

"I hope you like it. I think red will look good on you," Caio says, a gigantic smile on his face. I try to smile back and lower my eyes to look at the checkered shirt.

I feel my face burn and realize that if there were a contest between my face and this shirt to see which is the reddest, my face would definitely win the grand prize.

I try to process the idea that there exists in the world a color that looks good on me that's not black or gray. Red. I was wrong this whole time.

The house goes silent for a few seconds until my mom resumes her chatter all over again.

"Help me organize these bags, and, Felipe, order a pizza for us. I'm not getting in that kitchen today, not even to paint!"

She's laughing, and so is Caio. But this time I'm not jealous. I'm happy. Because the two of them are, officially, my favorite people in the world.

We have pizza for dinner and play three rounds of Uno (my mom wins twice, and Caio wins the other one), and it's late by the time I decide to retreat into my bedroom to sleep. I give up on the beige pajamas and am back to my old habits: old shorts and a Teenage Mutant Ninja Turtles T-shirt that I can't wear outside anymore because it has a hole under the armpit.

I leave the bedroom door open one more time, feeding the little bit of hope I still have in me. I don't know if it's luck, destiny, or Venus in the house of Mars, but for the first time in my life, things start to go the way I was hoping.

I'm lying in bed, checking what's new on Twitter, when I hear a slight knock on the door. I lift my head and see Caio standing there, holding a pillow and looking like an abandoned puppy.

I don't know what to say, so I keep staring at my phone and tweet my reaction: Houhfjkxhfdoduighl. Send tweet.

"So, um . . . Hi. Can I sleep here tonight? It's . . . the couch, you know? It—" Caio starts to explain himself.

"It's terrible. I know. You can say it," I interrupt, trying to sound funny. But I think my answer ends up sounding a bit rude, so I try to fix it by being cute: "Of course you can sleep here! It should have been that way from the beginning, but I . . . well, you know. I'm sorry. Make yourself comfortable. I'm sorry, again."

Caio just stands there looking at me, and I almost break out into a rendition of "Be Our Guest" from *Beauty and the Beast*, when I suddenly realize that I put away the guest mattress. I get up to pull out the retractable bed where Caio is going to sleep and apologize three more times. Two because I bump into him in the process and a third one for no apparent reason. I do all that in darkness because at no point did I realize that it might be a good idea to turn the lights back on. But Caio doesn't seem to mind.

When the guest bed is all set, I go back to my own bed and try to assume a position in which my belly won't flop to the side, so the hole in my shirt won't show. The room is still dark, so I honestly don't know why I even care. Caio throws the pillow onto the mattress, lies down, and lets out a sigh of relief. I can imagine him saying, "With god as my witness, I'll never sleep on that couch again!" like in that scene in *Gone with the Wind*.

But he doesn't say a thing.

Neither do I.

I keep staring at my phone screen. Surprisingly, I got two likes on my last tweet. I start typing "How to start a conversation" in Google, but even before I hit search, Caio breaks the silence.

"Thanks, Felipe."

"For the bed? I told you. It's fine."

"*Also* for the bed. But I meant the book. That you left for me. Thank you."

"Ah. Yes. *The Two Towers*. A good one. I hope you like it."

And there I am, thinking this would be another standard-issue dialogue in my collection of standard-issue dialogues with Caio, but he keeps going:

"I'll take good care of it, don't worry! It looks like it means a lot to you. It even has a personal dedication. Who's Thereza?"

"My grandmother. It was the last present she gave me before she died," I say, swallowing hard.

My grandmother, Thereza, would always give me books as Christmas and birthday presents. Most of them were classics that I never felt like reading, but after she was gone, I ended up reading all of them to feel closer to her. In all the books, she always wrote the same dedication:

Lipé,

The whole world is yours.

With love, Thereza

I always hated it when people called me Lipé, but when it was her, I didn't mind. My grandma gets permission.

The bedroom goes quiet again because, true to form, on the first opportunity I have for an actual conversation with Caio, I decide to bring up my dead grandmother.

"I'm sorry," Caio says in the softest voice.

I smile because I can tell that he's really sorry.

"It's okay. She'd love to know that someone borrowed the book. My grandma used to work at the library downtown. She spent her whole life helping people borrow books." Caio laughs a low laugh, and I don't know if it's the darkness in the bedroom or the fond memories of my grandmother, but I keep talking. "What did you think of the first book?"

"In general, I was surprised! I've always wanted to watch the movies, but I can't watch a movie unless I read the book first. It feels like cheating otherwise, y'know? So I grabbed the first book out of curiosity and I'm really liking it. Some parts are a little boring, but the story is awesome. I couldn't put it down! I just wonder what the second book is going to be like, now that Gandalf is dead."

I hold back a laugh, because if he hasn't watched the movies, he has no idea what's about to happen.

"When I read the books, I'd already seen all three movies, so there were no surprises for me. And yet, I cried when

Gandalf died because he's the best part of *The Lord of the Rings*," I say, and Caio laughs again.

I'm suddenly invaded by a good feeling—the kind you feel when you get the right answer twice on a BuzzFeed quiz.

"So you're the kind of person who likes the movie better than the book?" Caio asks with mock judgment in his voice.

"No, no!" I say right away. But then I stop to think and start to develop my arguments. "Though, to be honest, I think we're conditioned to say that the book is always better. But in reality . . . I don't know."

That's me, Mr. Articulate.

I reorganize my thoughts and continue, "I really like books. And I really like movies. Some good books are made into horrible movies, and great movies came from boring books. And the opposite is also true. I don't know. I like both. That's the worst answer, but it's what I have for you today."

Faced with the crappy case I've made, Caio lets out a final laugh, followed by a long yawn. It seems we're done talking for the night.

"Felipe, I think I'm going to sleep."

"Me too," I lie, because there's no way in hell I'll be able to turn around and fall sleep, knowing he's right here, lying next to me.

"Good night," we both say at almost the same time.

I look up at the ceiling and stare into the darkness while I wait for sleep to come. And that's when I notice something that I've never paid attention to before: Right in the corner of the bedroom, there's still one remaining glow-in-the-dark star sticker. I must not have noticed it when I removed all the others. But I have no doubt. It's almost not glowing anymore, but it's still there. One star on my bedroom ceiling. I know this is going to sound stupid, but I simply close my eyes and make a wish.

And three seconds later, I hear Caio calling my name.

"Felipe, can I ask you for something?"

I want to say, "A kiss? To hold hands? To profess my eternal love?!" But all that comes out of my mouth is "Yes?"

"What's the Wi-Fi password?"

I take a deep breath (a little frustrated, I have to admit) and answer, "merylstreep123, all lowercase."

I can see Caio smiling because the phone screen lights up his face when he enters the password. His smile is as intense as a thousand star stickers glowing in the dark and carries the satisfaction of someone who's just spent three whole days without knowing how to get onto the Wi-Fi.

"Okay, now good night," he says.

"See you tomorrow," I respond.

And the day after that. And the next, and the next.

DAY 4

I WAKE UP WITH SUNLIGHT coming in through my window, and the first thing I hear is Caio snoring. It's not a real snore; it's more like a purr. He doesn't sleep with his mouth open. His mouth is closed in a half smile, and it even seems like he knows he's being watched. I, on the other hand, have awful bedhead, my cheek is sticky with drool, and my shirt is rolled up to my midriff. I cover myself quickly, because I don't want him to see me like this.

"Good morning," Caio says when he wakes, his voice a little raspy.

I break into a cold sweat because, once again, I don't know how to act around him. Last night I did so well, but today is different. The room isn't dark anymore.

It doesn't matter that Caio isn't even looking at me; I still have this feeling that I'm being watched the whole time. I'm already used to all the looks that I get, but not to *his* look. I think I'll never get used to it. Because Caio's stare is more like a laser beam striking my body smack-dab in the middle, burning me alive as my organs slide out of my body. But in a good way.

"It's so nice to sleep on a real bed again!" Caio continues, since I didn't reply to his good morning.

"That's great" is all I can say.

Caio gives up on trying to sustain a conversation and starts exchanging texts on his phone with someone more interesting than me. Basically anybody.

We don't have time to stew in our awkward silence, because a few seconds later my mom knocks on the door and hurries into the room.

"Felipe, I have to teach today and I totally forgot, so there's no lunch for the two of you. Go to the supermarket and pick up something," she says, shoving some money in my face.

At the beginning of the year, my mom started volunteering at a nonprofit organization that helps low-income communities in our town. Every Monday she gives art lessons to a group of kids of all ages. It's not quite a *class*, because there are no exams, homework, or anything like that. My mom brings her own supplies and helps the kids create whatever they want. Paintings, sculptures, photos, collages. They learn a little bit of everything, and my mom always says that teaching makes her feel good.

I consider my options quickly. My mom spends the entire day at the organization and usually comes home late. Caio is still texting on his phone, and honestly, I don't know if I can stand an entire day like this.

"Can I come with you?" I ask, before she rushes out of the bedroom.

"What about Caio?" she asks.

"Hi!" he responds, peeling his eyes away from the phone. "Good morning, Rita! What about me?"

"Good morning, honey. I'm off to the community center. I teach art classes every Monday to a group of lovely kids—"

"I'm in!" he says, even before my mom finishes the sentence, and he seems pretty excited by the idea of not having to spend the entire day alone with me.

"Go on, get ready, then, the two of you. I'm already late!" my mom says, clapping her hands.

Two seconds later, Caio is already up. Taking off his shirt. In front of me. The scene doesn't happen in slow motion with a sax solo in the background. It's all very quick and natural, as if he were already used to taking off his shirt like this, in front of someone.

Caio puts on a clean shirt, and when he takes off his pajama shorts to get into his jeans, I forget how breathing works. Because for one second my eyes meet Caio's underwear (black boxers), and my mom is still standing in the doorway. And this is, without a doubt, the weirdest moment of my entire life.

"I'm ready," says Caio, a smile on his face, as if he expects an award for getting dressed in record time.

The two of them stare at me, waiting for me to do the same. And, of course, I won't. I'd rather leave the house in my Teenage Mutant Ninja Turtles shirt with a hole in the armpit than change in front of Caio.

So that's exactly what I do. I put on a fleece jacket over the old T-shirt, and pants over the shorts I'm wearing, as if it were the most normal thing in the whole world, and a few seconds later, I'm ready, too.

"All right! Now, let's go!" my mom says, slapping my butt.

As if this morning needed to get *any* weirder.

"Can I keep the cash?" I ask, holding up the twenty she handed me earlier.

"Keep dreaming, Felipe." With that, she snaps it out of my hands and kisses my cheek.

*

We get on a crowded bus but find two empty seats in the back. My mom and Caio take them while I'm left standing, because bus seats were not made for anyone who's a little larger than the norm. In fact, there are *lots* of things in the world that were not made for fat people. Bathroom stalls, school desks, and cool clothes are just a few good examples.

"The people I meet at the community center lead such different lives from one another that every week I feel like I'm learning more than I'm teaching, you know?" my mom says

52

to Caio about the kids. "There are toddlers who lost their parents to drugs, and big kids who can barely spell their own names. There's a fourteen-year-old girl who arrived last week, and when I asked what she wanted to learn, she said she was just dropping off her kid. The girl has a one-year-old son! The cutest baby in the world, but still. It's a hard life. Having a child so early forces you to learn things that you shouldn't be old enough to learn."

I can hear the emotion in her voice, and Caio is listening so intently he barely blinks. That's my mom's superpower. When she gets serious, everyone stops to listen.

"I know I'm not teaching these kids a trade. They spend the afternoon playing with glitter glue and Play-Doh. And let's be honest, art isn't paying anyone's bills, you know? If it did, you would be sleeping in a decent guest room, am I right, Caio?" she jokes, and the three of us laugh. "But I like to think that when they spend the day with me, they're safe. These kids live surrounded by violence, drugs, and abuse. That's their normal, and I know I can't protect all of them, but sometimes art can," she says, and I can see a tear running down her left cheek.

Caio looks at me as if he doesn't know how to react, so I grab my mom's hand and squeeze it tight, because I think it's the right thing to do, and Caio holds her other hand. She brings both our hands to her lips and gives each one a kiss.

It is a beautiful moment, but it would be better if we weren't in a crowded bus. And if I weren't wearing briefs and an old pair of shorts under my jeans. Seriously, *why* did I think this was a good idea?

✻

After almost an hour on the bus, we finally arrive at the community center. It's basically a two-story house with a very humble design. As soon as we walk in, we're welcomed by a tiny woman with a colorful scarf over her hair.

"Good morning, Rita! Your class is already waiting for you," the lady says, hugging my mom.

"I brought my son along today, Carol," my mom replies, and Carol looks at Caio right away.

"What a good-looking fellow!" she says, hugging him. Carol is definitely a hugger.

"Ah, no. I'm not her son, just the neighbor," Caio says, a little embarrassed.

"Hi, nice to meet you. I'm Felipe," I chime in, bracing for the hug.

But Carol only offers her hand to shake mine, a tight smile on her face.

I don't have a lot of time to analyze the situation, because my mom is already pulling us down the hallway. The center is way bigger than it looks from the outside. The hallway is full of doors, and each one has a little sign indicating a different class. Ballet, music, jujitsu, drama . . . They have everything in this place. But I'm relieved when I find the door I've been looking for since I first set foot in this place—the bathroom.

"Gotta go to the bathroom, see you in the classroom," I say, making my way toward the door with a sign that says BOYS.

"Last door on the right down this same hallway," my mom says, moving on to her first class of the day. Caio goes after her.

The bathroom is small, but it has what I need. A stall. Putting jeans over my shorts was, by far, the worst idea I have ever had. And I have a pretty big collection of bad ideas.

I go into a stall, drop my pants, and take a relieved breath. I have a heat rash on my legs (sorry to throw this unexpected information at you, but hold tight because this is an important bit of the story), and I just sit on the toilet for a while, trying to figure out how to bring the shorts with me to the classroom and hide them in my mom's purse. Then I hear the bathroom door open and some boys walk in, making a racket. I sit there in silence because I don't want to be caught with my pants down. Literally.

"Stop—please! I didn't do anything to you!" I hear a kid's

voice say. The boy can't be more than eight. Or maybe ten. I'm not an expert on kids.

"Gonna cry, little girl?" I hear an older kid answer while a group of boys laughs.

"Why don't you face me yourself, then?" says the younger one, braver than I was when I was his age.

"Because you're fat! We need more than one to handle all of you!" another older boy answers, and the others start laughing harder. Then one by one they start launching attacks at the younger boy:

"Jabba the Hutt!"

"Tub of lard!"

"Land whale!"

And for a second, it feels as if they're talking to me. Like I said, I'm used to it, but hearing these words being said to a child, one after the other like a reflex, makes my blood boil.

I've never been brave. I've always been the kind of person who takes it in stride and pretends nothing ever happened. But this time, I pull my pants up (now without the shorts) and open the stall door with a bang to scare the boys. I find the younger boy pressed against a corner of the bathroom and surrounded by five older kids. They must be around thirteen.

"What's going on here?" I say, making my voice as serious

as I can. I think I can make myself seem like an adult, at least enough to frighten them.

"Nothing!" one of the boys says. At the same time, all of them get away from the younger boy and run out of the bathroom. I am overcome with relief, because walking out of the stall and confronting them was my only plan.

"Thanks, mister," the younger boy says in a very low voice. His eyes are full of tears, and it breaks my heart.

I smile to show him everything is fine, and also because I think it's funny that he's calling me *mister*.

"You can call me Felipe," I say, stepping closer to the boy and crouching next to him. "What's your name?"

"Eddie," the boy says, still shy. "It's João Eduardo, but they call me Eddie."

Eddie is a bigger boy, and his clothes don't fit him anymore. His old T-shirt is tight, and it lets a good chunk of his belly out.

"How old are you, Eddie?" I ask, because I don't know what else to say.

"Nine."

I was so close!

"You were brave, standing up to those boys. They're jerks!" I say, and then regret it immediately, because I don't know if it's appropriate to say the word *jerks* to a nine-year-old.

"They always do that. I'm used to it by now," Eddie says, then punches the wall.

I can feel the anger in his words, and more than that, I can identify with him in a way I've never identified with anyone before. It's as if, at nine years old, Eddie is already fed up with the world. All of a sudden, I understand how my mom feels when she says she wishes she could keep all her students safe.

I try to change the subject. "Which class are you taking here?"

"Art. With Ms. Rita," he says, and it makes me happy that I get to help make this kid feel safe for the entire day.

"I'm going to the art class, too! Shall we?" I say, then put my hands in my jacket pockets because I don't know if I'm supposed to hold his hand.

I think when they're nine, kids don't hold adults' hands anymore. But to my astonishment, Eddie nods and holds out his hand to me.

*

If you think spending the day surrounded by kids painting canvases and creating Play-Doh figurines is an easy task, you are completely mistaken. These kids are little devils who scream the whole time and run around in every direction, and it's impossible to get one second of peace in the classroom. But every time a student calls my mom over to show her the piece they've created, I can see in her smile that the effort is well worth it.

Some kids get here, stay for half an hour, and then leave, whereas some spend the whole day at the center. Eddie is the type who spends the day here. From the moment we walked out of the bathroom, he hasn't left my side. He walked around the classroom introducing me to his friends, and all of them seemed fascinated, as if Eddie had made the most incredible discovery of all time.

"Who could imagine you'd be so good with kids, huh, Felipe?" my mom remarks when she sees me sitting in a circle with Eddie and three other children. "Want me to bring my son every week?" she asks them.

And they all start yelling excitedly, jumping on me.

Caio is doing well, too. He has a group of older kids building sculptures with Play-Doh, Popsicle sticks, and paint. Surrounded by so many people, the two of us haven't been alone for a single moment, but we've exchanged laughs whenever a kid says something funny.

By the end of the afternoon, I'm dead tired. We organize a little gallery in the classroom with the paintings and sculptures by all the students, then start saying our goodbyes to the kids, who begin to trickle out. Some are still ambling around the hallways because they simply have nowhere to go.

Caio and I help my mom clean up the classroom before we

leave, and when we get to the front entrance, I hear Eddie call my name.

"Mr. Felipe! Hold on!" He comes rushing down the hallway, and when he finally reaches us, he needs a moment to catch his breath.

"I made this for you!" He hands me a piece of paper. It's a makeshift envelope with something written in a kid's handwriting.

From: João Eduardo

To: Mr. Felipe

When I unfold the envelope, my smile feels too big to fit on my face.

"Do you like it, mister?" Eddie asks, standing on the tips of his toes so he can see the paper in my hand.

It's a drawing of me in a Batman costume, flying in a blue sky full of clouds. Technically, Batman can't fly, but of course I'm not about to tell him that. I love the drawing, anyway. I'm still fat in Eddie's version of me, but my arms are strong and muscular. It's one of the coolest things anyone has ever made for me.

"I think it's awesome, Eddie! Thank you so much. I'll keep it forever!" I say, patting his head.

He lets out a laugh that rings happily in my ears, and I feel like I should give him something in exchange for the drawing.

I shove my hand in my jacket pocket and find a chocolate bar. I have no idea how long it has been lost in there, but even so, it seems good enough to eat.

"Do you like chocolate?" I ask, handing him the half-melted bar.

"Yay! Thanks!" He starts unwrapping the candy excitedly.

"Don't tell anyone else, but you were my favorite. I'll come back another day so we can draw some more, deal?"

Eddie gives me a thumbs-up and says something I can't make out because he's chewing. Then he turns around and runs off. I fold my gift back into its envelope and put it in my pocket where the chocolate bar was, and when I look at my mom, she's all emotional.

"This is why I come back every week," she whispers in my ear as she, Caio, and I walk to the bus stop.

✽

When we get home, we're all exhausted. The first thing I do is run to my room and hang my present up on the wall. I have a mural made up of my favorite superhero posters over my desk, and the drawing of me as Batman just claimed its space. To be honest, I don't even care about Batman that much, but this drawing is awesome.

In case you're wondering (which you probably aren't), these are my top three favorite superheroes of all time:

1. **Green Lantern**, because he has a ring that can turn him into ANYTHING—literally—and to me, that's the coolest superpower ever. This, obviously, doesn't take into account the movie starring Ryan Reynolds as the Green Lantern, because that movie was one of the worst things ever created by mankind, right after Chicken & Waffles Lay's.

2. **Robin**, who's technically a sidekick and doesn't have any superpowers, but I love him and this is *my* list.

3. **Aquaman**, because he's the closest a super-hero can get to being a mermaid.

We eat leftover pizza together in the living room, but today the TV is off. We're all too worn-out to look for the remote.

"Caio, don't even *think* about telling your mother that I let you eat pizza two days in a row, do you hear me?" my mom says.

Caio promises he can keep it a secret and, when he finishes his slice, excuses himself to go shower.

I'm alone in the living room with my mom, and she rests her head on my shoulder.

"I loved spending the day with you, son. You did so well!" She steals an olive from my slice of pizza. "I've never seen João Eduardo so happy. He's always been a quiet kid who won't talk to anybody. I thought it was so strange when I saw him run into the classroom with you in tow."

"Sometimes people only need someone else to start the conversation," I say, because that's what I have been hoping for every single day since Caio arrived.

My mom seems absorbed in her thoughts for a minute, as if choosing which words to use, and suddenly she blurts out a question as if it is a confession.

"Felipe, you're happy, aren't you?"

"Most of the time, yeah. I am happy," I answer. Which is technically true. But I'm not in the mood to open up and spill my heart to my mom. Not right now, anyway.

"Most of the time is a good chunk of time, isn't it?"

"I think so."

"And the rest of the time, when you're not happy, you know you can talk to me, don't you?"

"I know," I say, uncertain of where she's going with this conversation. "Anyway, today was fun and all, but now I need, like, twenty hours of sleep to recover from it."

"Good night, son. Mommy loves you," she says, still pensive.

I kiss my mom good night and take a quick and lazy shower, and when I get to the bedroom, Caio is already in bed, wearing his naval pajamas and reading the first few pages of *The Two Towers*.

"You can turn off the lights if you want. I won't be able to read for much longer," he says.

I turn them off and get in bed, and suddenly all the sleep in me is gone. Now that we're in the dark, the confident and talkative Felipe takes over.

"So, what did you think of today?" I ask.

"It was fun! At first I thought it'd be overwhelming with all those kids, y'know?" Caio answers. "But in the end, it was totally worth it."

"That's what my mom always says. She loves those kids. Some days she talks about her kids so much that I even get a little jealous!" (Seriously.)

"Ah, but I would, too. Your mom is incredible! When she took me to the mall yesterday, we talked so much. I've never felt that comfortable, not even with my own mom!" Caio says.

I feel a little sorry for him and don't know how to keep the conversation going, because honestly, what am I going to say to a guy who doesn't like his own mother?

"It's not that I don't *like* my mom," Caio adds, as if reading my thoughts. "It's just that sometimes she can be so . . . complicated."

"Complicated how?"

"She's way overprotective. I mean, I'm seventeen years old and spending my vacation at my neighbor's house because she doesn't trust me enough to leave me home by myself. I tried to negotiate, promised to call their hotel room every night to check in, but it was no use. By the way, I guess I never apologized for that, huh? Sorry I ruined your vacation. I doubt you'd choose to spend fifteen days locked up with me."

You have no idea, Caio.

"Oh, come on! It's all good. It's not as if I had loads of plans," I say with a smile, even though I know that Caio can't see it in the dark. "It's just that my mom only told me you were staying with us about three minutes before you got here."

Caio laughs.

"You see?" I go on. "She's not the perfect mom you're imagining. Ms. Rita is a fraud!"

"I don't know about that, but I can tell how much she loves you," Caio says, and I find it so weird to hear someone else talk about my mom's feelings for me. "For real, Felipe. Yesterday at the mall, she would only talk about you. About how responsible you are, and that you're such good company, and great at choosing movies and guessing who will be eliminated from cooking competitions on TV."

I feel proud because I am actually really good at that, and it's nice to get a little recognition sometimes.

"But you know, that's a mom thing. I bet yours also loves

telling other people about you. They're all like that!" I say, trying to make him feel better.

"I don't know. Sometimes I think she's ashamed of me."

"Why would she be *ashamed* of you?" I ask with genuine indignation in my voice.

"Because I'm gay," Caio says, and in that moment the air in my room feels lighter.

Let's make something clear. Knowing Caio is gay doesn't come as a shock to me. I have good gaydar and have always known this to be true. I've seen Caio's Instagram about twenty million times. I know what kind of music he listens to, where he hangs out, and even what filters he uses for his selfies.

And to be honest, I think that if Caio were straight, I wouldn't be so in love with him. I like boys who are obviously gay because *I* am obviously gay, and dream of someone with whom I can be obviously gay together. I'm not super attracted to the straight-acting types (with a few exceptions, like Hugh Jackman).

And yet, hearing Caio say *I AM GAY* makes it all feel so . . . *official.* You know when Ricky Martin came out of the closet and everyone was surprised, not that he was gay but that he decided to say so? And all of a sudden, it was way cooler to listen to "Livin' La Vida Loca" because Ricky Martin was *officially* gay? That's how I feel right now.

So, without any shame, I just put the truth out there.

"I am, too. Gay, that is."

"Yeah, I figured," Caio responds, almost immediately.

I've never talked to another gay boy my age (unless you count the internet), and suddenly I have a million questions to ask. They appear one after the other in my head, and I feel like I might explode.

"Does your mom know?" is the first one I ask.

"She does. I've never said it out loud, but I've also never hidden it. I think it's kind of obvious. I don't know. And she always says things like 'Stop waving your hands so much when you talk, Caio' or 'Sit like a man, Caio.' So, yeah, she knows but pretends she doesn't. Like I said, she's complicated. Yours?"

"She knows. I told her."

"Really? And how did it go?" Caio is so interested he plops on his elbows to hear about it.

"It's not a very exciting story. I said, 'Mom, there's something I need to tell you. I'm gay. Please love me.' Then she said she had always known and it was all right, and she would love me forever, et cetera," I say, but this is a very condensed version of the story.

Like everything else in my life, the real story was a little more dramatic.

It happened last year, when I bought the teen magazine

with tips to get over your body-image insecurities. After realizing that an article in a stupid magazine wasn't going to be of any help, I cried a little, but the crying got out of control, and suddenly I was crying *hard*. Sobbing, drooling, and making noise. My mom, who was painting in the kitchen, heard me cry and ran to the bedroom to see what was the matter. I'd felt so ashamed! Ashamed of my body, of my crying, and especially of my mom seeing all of that. I didn't know how to explain it to her. I could have said, "So, Mom, as you might have noticed, I'm fat. At school, fat people aren't the popular ones, and in general, everything sucks." But I didn't. I was afraid of saying it.

My attempt to hide one secret ended with me revealing another one. Still with my eyes full of tears, I said, "Mom, there's something I need to tell you. I'm gay. Please love me," and she cried, hugged me, and promised to love me forever. In the end, I went to bed happy that night. It was a weight off my shoulders, and ever since, being gay has never been a problem.

Of course, I'm not about to tell Caio the full story on the second night we share a bedroom. But he seems satisfied by the short version, and after some time in silence, I hear his voice really low:

"I hope one day my mom will love me like that, too." It sounds a little sad, as if he's about to burst into tears at any moment. I want to hug him, because that's what you do for someone who's about to cry, right?

But I don't have the courage.

"Don't be silly. She's your mom. She's loved you from the second you were born," I say, and hope these words are enough to make him feel hugged.

After that, Caio doesn't say anything else, and I stay quiet until sleep comes.

DAY 5

I WAKE UP TO CAIO'S voice whispering to someone on the phone. I don't want to interrupt, so I pretend to still be asleep. I know it's not right to eavesdrop on someone else's conversation, but I don't know what to do, and I'm too sleepy to think of a way out of it.

"Yes, Mom. I told you, everything is fine, the food is good, I'm showering every day, and my clean clothes will last until you're back," he whispers into his phone, and I notice a slight annoyance in his voice.

The call isn't on speaker, but I can still hear his mom on the other side. I can't understand every single word, but she seems annoyed as well. She's always been that type of person. The type who yells.

"All right, all right. As soon as Rita is up, I'll ask her to give you a call. But really, Mom, there's no need for that, I'm not a child—" He gets interrupted, and his mom continues to talk without taking a breath.

Suddenly, she says something that makes Caio exhale impatiently. Apparently, his mom can hear that, too, because right afterward he starts to explain himself.

"No, Mom, I'm not huffing. Look, it's too early. I'll talk to you later. Everything is fine. Enjoy your trip, and if you want to talk to me, just text!" And without bothering to whisper now, he says, "No need to call!" then hangs up.

I must have given up on pretending to sleep, and when I realize it, Caio is looking at me as I stare at the ceiling.

"Sorry if I woke you up," he says. "My mom wanted to call because, according to her, she needs to hear my voice to know that I'm fine. Because the two hundred texts she sends every day aren't enough." Caio laughs briefly, but I can still see that he's nervous.

"No worries, I was already half-awake," I say. "My mom is like that, too. She sends me a thousand messages when I'm not around. You should have seen it when she discovered emojis!"

Caio laughs, and I feel like a dirty liar, because of course that's not true (except for the emoji part, since my mom loves to overuse them). She never texts me out of worry when I'm not around because A) she's not like that, and B) I'm always around. But for some reason, I think that pointing out some of my mom's flaws might make Caio like his better. And—I know, I know—that makes absolutely no sense.

"Moms," he says with a sigh.

"Aye, aye," I say, because I have no idea how else to continue this conversation.

And then we lie there in silence, doing stuff on our phones, and I wonder how people used to avoid awkward silence before smartphones where invented.

*

Next to Cake Saturdays, Tuesdays are my favorite day of the week, because that's when I get to meet with Olivia. A few weeks after I came out to my mom, she suggested I start going to therapy. At the time, I was a little scared because I wasn't sure if she was trying to "cure" me, or if she thought I was crazy. She patiently explained to me that going to therapy doesn't mean I'm crazy.

"By the way, a lot of people develop issues precisely because they're *not* in therapy," she said, laughing.

Talking to Olivia always makes me feel so good that I wait anxiously for Tuesdays. Therapy isn't like cold medicine, where you take one pill and then feel better the next day. I remember the first time I met Olivia, thinking she was going to give me all the secrets to a happy life and I'd walk out of our session magically thin and hot. That's not how it works; it's a long journey. But trust me, this story would be twice as dramatic and three times more self-deprecating if it weren't for my therapist.

I leave right after lunch, and when I get to her office,

Olivia is waiting for me with the same smile she always wears. She's Black and the tallest woman I've ever seen in my life. Her thick curls are always wrapped in a different way with a scarf, and her clothes are always very elegant.

I've never asked about her age because I don't think there's ever a right time to ask, "So, how old are you?" But I suspect she's about fortysomething. She doesn't look like she's in her forties, but more like someone who tells you she's forty and then you're surprised because you would've guessed thirty.

Olivia's office is small but very cozy. There's no chaise longue like in the movies (to my disappointment), but there's a big, comfortable armchair. I don't feel as large sitting on it.

On the wall next to the window, there's a shelf with a bunch of knickknacks. Most of them are little dolls sitting on a couch near a little sign that says PSYCHOLOGY. Of all of them, only one is Black. I guess that says a lot about the knickknacks industry.

"So, Felipe, how has your week been?" Olivia asks after welcoming me and offering water, coffee, and yogurt hard candy.

I pop a candy in my mouth as I think of where to start.

This week has been a whirlwind because nothing ever happens in my life, and then suddenly everything happened. In our sessions, I usually talk about my problems in school,

73

or about how I managed not to cry for four days straight. But today I have a lot to say. So I spill it all out.

I tell her about Caio staying with us and how his presence makes me feel completely desperate. I tell her about how awful I felt when he saw me wrapped in the towel. I think about mentioning Caio in his pajamas, how it's the most gorgeous sight in the world, but I leave that part out because it's the kind of stuff that sounds ridiculous in your head but even more ridiculous when you say it out loud. I decide to keep Caio-in-pajamas all to myself. Instead, I tell her about the red shirt he picked out for me, and how I'd like nothing more than to talk to him about any and all things, but I can't because I always end up deciding that I don't have anything interesting to say.

"Whoa," Olivia says as she looks at her notes. "A lot's happened in the last few days, hasn't it? But let's take it one step at a time. First of all, I'm so proud of your evolution, Felipe. You were able to talk to your neighbor, and that's wonderful!"

The difficulty I have socializing with others my own age is something we've worked on together since our first session.

"But our conversations are short, and he probably thinks I'm weird," I answer, refusing to accept her compliments.

"One step at a time, Felipe," she repeats. "This first interaction between the two of you is important, because if you're open to dialogue, that means something. Do you feel comfortable around Caio?" she asks, her hand on her chin as if she were Sherlock Holmes interrogating a suspect.

"Sometimes I do, sometimes I don't," I respond.

"When do you, and when don't you?"

"We talk at night. Before bed. But in the morning, I can't say anything. I freeze and just end the conversation with an 'aye, aye'," I say, frustrated.

"And do you know why that is?" Olivia asks, and I already know where she's going.

"I think I do. In fact, I'm almost positive I do. At night, in the dark, I feel safer. Because he can't see me."

"That's an interesting conclusion," she says. "And do you intend to spend the next few days talking to Caio only at night and ignoring him during the day?"

"No, no!" I say, a little loud, maybe trying to convince myself more than her. "I want to talk to him the whole day. In a healthy way, of course. You get what I mean."

She laughs a little, and I keep talking.

"I don't know what's up with me. When I look at him, the words don't come out right. But in the dark, I can talk without thinking about it."

"Felipe, I have an exercise for you this week," she says, and I roll my eyes, because I fail most of the exercises she gives me.

Olivia has given me a number of them. They're like

challenges that I have to accomplish every week, usually silly things, such as saying good morning to a classmate who has never spoken to me, or taking a different route to class. Others are harder, like not staring at the floor when the guys at school call me names.

"You're going to try and establish a dialogue with Caio, and you have to be the one to start the conversation. In the daytime. Do you think you can do it?"

"Yes," I lie.

"It doesn't have to be a two-hour conversation, but try hard to voice your opinion about a topic. Show how you really feel. Don't try to shape your opinion to what you think Caio wants to hear. Be honest," she instructs, and I think I should probably ask her for a pen and a piece of paper to write down all the rules of this challenge.

I miss the good ole days when the exercise of the week was to talk with a mirror.

"Okay, Olivia, I swear I'll try hard. But I never know where to start. I don't know how to begin a conversation, and it always makes me so anxious. Once, I even looked up 'How to start a conversation' on Google! It was no use, though; the results sucked," I say, and my drama is so genuine that I don't even feel guilty for using the word *sucked* in therapy.

"Felipe, don't be afraid of starting the wrong conversation.

If that happens, you can try again another time. Talking about things you both like is interesting, but to be honest, I'm personally much more interested in hearing about experiences that aren't my own. Conversations that teach us new things are the best ones," she says, and I write down that sentence in my head, because it's good. "What do the two of you have in common?"

I consider it for a second, and then start a list.

"We're both seventeen. We are both gay . . ." and I can't think of anything else.

"Okay, and what is it that the two of you *don't* have in common?"

"Ah, that's an easy one! We don't go to the same school. I'm fat and he's not. My mom is wonderful, and his mom . . . well, she's a bit much," I say with a quick laugh.

"Very good. Give that some more thought on your way home. Think about ways to open up and show him your opinions about things. But don't forget that this exercise is about you, and not about Caio. What will determine your success in this exercise is your willingness to have a conversation, not Caio's opinion about what you talk about. Are we good for today?" she asks, getting up from her chair. That's her way of saying that our time is up.

Olivia walks me to the door, and before I walk out, she puts her hand on my shoulder.

"Felipe, one last thing. When you're talking, don't hold back your smile. You look good when you smile."

I don't really know how to process that information, so I answer with a question.

"Now you're giving me tips on how to flirt, too?"

She laughs. "Just this once. I won't charge you for that one. And, for god's sake, you're seventeen years old! Don't use the word *flirt*. No one talks like that anymore."

I leave her office with a smile, but it fades away after two minutes, because I realize that I will, inevitably, fail this week's exercise.

*

I spend the next few hours trying as hard as I can not to go straight home. I take a walk in the town park, but there's nothing new to see: the same retired gentlemen playing chess, the same pigeons eating bread crumbs by the lake, the same children running after said pigeons, who—poor things—can't eat their bread crumbs in peace.

I try to turn each scene I observe into a possible conversation topic with Caio. Most of the ideas I have are very bad, but organizing my thoughts like this helps me keep my anxiety in check.

In a town as small as mine, it's hard to take the scenic route anywhere. Everything is way too close.

I go to a newsstand, read some comics, and leave without

getting anything. I go to the bookstore and buy a book I don't need. I go to a coffee shop and read at a table by the corner until an employee starts giving me the stink eye because it's been over two hours and all I got was an iced tea. I don't have money to buy anything else because I spent it all at the bookstore, so I decide I can't avoid going home forever. Also it's late and I'm starving.

When I finally get home, my mom doesn't seem to notice that it took me an extra four hours to go to the therapist this time. Caio's mom probably would have contacted the FBI, but my mom isn't like that. She and Caio are laughing and talking in the kitchen while she cooks dinner and he does the dishes.

We haven't set the table to eat in the kitchen since Caio first got here. Tonight is no different. The three of us eat in the living room, sitting on the flowery couch, watching TV. The couch is small (especially when you consider the fact that I take up the space of two people), but when I'm there with the two of them, I feel comfortable.

My mom tells me she spent the afternoon painting with Caio, and they start laughing when she says that, unfortunately, he doesn't have the talent for it.

I enjoy their company, but I don't say much during dinner. All I want is to go to my room, turn off the lights, and wait until Caio comes in so we can talk.

And believe it or not, that's exactly what I do.

It's not even ten p.m., and I'm already in bed. The room is dark, and the door is ajar. Of course, Caio doesn't come right away, because no one goes to bed this early. Still, I just lie there and wait. I watch my usual YouTube videos, see on Twitter that they're making yet another *Transformers* movie (either the sixth or seventh, I've lost count), and tweet my thoughts about it: Who asked for another transformers????????

I get distracted enough that I'm surprised when Caio walks into the room quietly. I think he just got out of the shower, because the room is suddenly filled with the smell of his soap. That's right, he brought his own soap, and now I'm used to his smell in the bathroom. But here, in my room, it dominates every nook and cranny. It makes me want to pounce on his neck.

"Hey," I say in a low voice when he closes the door.

He jumps but recovers quickly.

"Oh, hey! I thought you were asleep," Caio says, lying on the mattress next to my bed.

"I was just tired but not sleepy. It was a long day," I try to say in an exhausted voice, but I'm a terrible actor.

"Where did you go all day?" Caio asks, more out of politeness than out of curiosity.

"Therapy."

And then I was killing time by wandering around town because I didn't want to come back and face you while the lights were still on, I think.

"For real?" Caio seems much more interested now. "At the beginning of the year, I told my mom that I wanted to go to therapy. But she didn't think it was a good idea. She said it's for crazy people and that I'm totally normal."

I'm glad it's dark and Caio can't see my eye roll. Because, seriously, what is wrong with his mother?

"But therapy isn't for crazy people! In fact, there are lots of people who develop mental health issues because they're *not* in therapy," I quote my mom, indignant, as if Caio's mom could hear me.

"Did therapy help you with being, you know . . . gay?" Caio asks in a whisper.

I think about it for a moment and realize that, in the last few months, my being gay has rarely ever come up in my sessions with Olivia. I never have issues talking about it. I've always known I am gay, that I can't change, and I don't *want* to. My mom accepts me, I accept myself, and that's the end of it. In our sessions, I mostly talk about my shyness, my weight, and how people see me. Being gay is always a smaller detail compared to my truckload of crises.

"It helped me a little with being gay at the beginning. But now it helps me with a bunch of other stuff. Shyness. Anxiety.

That kind of stuff," I answer quickly, opening up to Caio more than I'd like to.

He just ponders for a few seconds. He seems to be deciding what to do with the information that I go to therapy to help with my shyness.

"It's funny because we used to be friends, remember? When we were kids," he finally says. "Then you disappeared, never came down to play at the pool anymore, and I remember being really upset. As we got older, you'd always just kind of stick to your corner, and I had a lot of doubts. I wasn't sure if you were shy or just a jerk. Then as soon as I got here on that first day, you yelled at me. And in that moment, I had no more doubts. I thought, *He really is just a jerk.*"

I swallow hard and Caio hears it, because he continues talking hurriedly.

"Wait, let me finish! Then we started talking, and I don't think you're a jerk anymore, I swear! You're just shy, that's all. Sometimes it's hard to tell the difference."

I take a relieved breath.

"How can you tell the difference?" I ask. "Between being shy and being a jerk, I mean."

"It's not easy," Caio answers in a funny voice, as if he were an expert on the subject. "It's all in the details. The day I got here, for instance. Early that morning, when I was on my way to school, you came into the elevator and said good morning. Jerks don't say good morning."

"So you're saying *you're* a jerk, because if I recall correctly, you didn't answer me!" I say, laughing.

Caio laughs, too, and in the dim light filtering through the windows I can see him raise his hands over his head, as if he were surrendering after being caught red-handed.

"Fine, fine. I *was* a jerk in the elevator. I had just argued with my mom about spending the next fifteen days here. It was my last attempt at convincing her that I could stay home by myself. Obviously, she said no. I was so mad when I left . . ." Caio tries to justify. "I'm sorry. I swear I am the kind of person who responds to people on the elevator."

"I would like to accept your apology, but I need proof."

"Well, I'll show you proof!" Caio says, getting up from his bed.

For a second, I think he'll jump on me and kiss me intensely, and then our love will be official. But obviously that's not what he does. He reaches for his phone and sends a voice message to someone I don't know.

"Becky, emergency! I need your help to prove that I'm not a jerk. So as soon as you can, I need you to send me a testimonial about how wonderful it is to be my friend. But please try hard; it needs to be convincing! I need to show my neighbor that I'm an amazing human being. Thanks, see you soon, bye!" he says into his phone.

I am a little upset that I'm just the "neighbor" instead of something else.

A few seconds later, Caio gets a response. He hits play and I hear a girl say, "Hey, Caio's neighbor, don't believe this kid. His face might be cute, but his soul is cruel. He complains about everything, always shows up late, and wears Crocs and thinks they're cool. Bye—" The recording stops before she finishes her farewell. I'm laughing as I imagine Caio in Crocs. Caio is laughing, too, because his plan backfired.

"Becky is my best friend. And I'm sure she's trying to sabotage me because she's jealous."

His phone beeps, announcing another audio message. He hits play and Becky's voice invades our bedroom again.

"The last message was a joke. Except for the thing about the Crocs, which is totally true. Caio is wonderful, gives great advice, makes a divine brigadeiro, and has three years of experience as an underwear model. Okay, that last part isn't true. But, hey, just to be clear, *I* am his best friend, and therefore THAT POSITION IS NO LONGER AVAILABLE. There, I said it, bye."

"You see?" Caio points at me. "I'm not a jerk. There's your proof."

"I still have my doubts about the Crocs part," I say, evaluating the situation.

"Dude, Crocs are basically slippers that you can wear outdoors. Why *not* wear them?" he counters, and deep down, I think it might make sense.

"Oh, and about the brigadeiro. I'm interested," I say, thinking about the perfect mix of condensed milk, cocoa powder, and butter, then regret it almost immediately.

Because I hate talking about food. Because when you're fat and you talk about food, people always think, *There goes fatty, talking about food!* But Caio doesn't seem to even think about that. He looks excited and promises to make brigadeiro tomorrow.

We spend some more time talking, and I learn a bunch of random facts about him. He's allergic to honey, he broke the same arm three times when he was a kid, and he didn't learn how to ride a bike until last year. I tell him random stuff about me, too. I like popcorn with no salt, no butter, no nothing. Just pure popcorn that tastes like Styrofoam. I've never broken a bone in my body but always wanted to have a cast so I could pretend to be a cyborg—half boy, half robot. I tried to give myself a haircut once and it was the worst decision I've ever made in my entire life.

We stay up late sharing stories and minor facts about ourselves. We take turns, and I never feel like I'm talking too much or too little. When we decide it's finally time to go to bed, I fall asleep feeling more comfortable than ever and believing that tomorrow will be a great day to win my therapy challenge. Having a conversation with Caio is the easiest thing in the world!

DAY 6

HAVING A CONVERSATION WITH CAIO is the hardest thing in the world!

I don't know why, but when he looks at me, I can barely talk. I suddenly forget how to organize my words and form complete sentences. I feel silly most of the time.

We woke up today to the sound of rain. Caio started talking about the weather, and I mumbled something back and stared at the ceiling.

Then this afternoon, I tried twice to approach him and start talking. The first time, I made a comment about the rain, then noticed we'd already covered that subject. Caio laughed and tried to continue our small talk, but I pretended I had to go to the bathroom and stayed in there for a while. The second time, I thought about asking how things were going at his school, but then I saw that he was focused on reading the book I lent him, so I gave up.

Before she left to deliver some paintings to a gallery downtown, my mom asked if we really planned on spending the whole day locked inside the apartment. Caio and I looked out the window at the same time and nodded without saying a word.

And now here we are, alone at home, sitting in the living room. Caio is still reading, more focused than ever, and I decide to do the same. I grab the book I bought yesterday after therapy and pick up reading where I left off.

It's a fantasy novel about a girl who was raised like any other person until, on her seventeenth birthday, she discovers she has special powers and a mysterious past. Now shit's hitting the fan all throughout the kingdom, and everyone's future lies in the hands of this girl who doesn't know how to control her powers and doesn't even try to learn how to. Have you ever read a book like this? Because I've read about fifteen.

I can't focus on the story and spend more time leafing through the pages than actually reading.

"Is your book any good?" Caio asks.

He's lying on the couch, and I'm propped against the pillows on the floor near the carpet. I take a deep breath before answering.

"One of the worst I've ever read in my life," I say. Caio laughs and contorts his body to get a peek at the cover.

We go back to sitting in silence, but suddenly Caio stands up and positions himself right in front of me.

"I need to ask you something, but don't answer unless you want to," he says, and I feel my body go cold.

I hug the pillow that I was using to hide my belly, and only after a few seconds have passed do I realize that Caio is waiting on me for a response. I nod, and that's enough for him.

"Why have you been so quiet all day? Is it something I've done?"

I don't know what to say, and I need some time to think. I expected he might question me about it sooner or later, but I wasn't smart enough to have an answer waiting for him.

"It's not you; it's me," I say in a very low and ashamed voice, because honestly, what a crappy answer!

"Just last night we had this long conversation, but when we woke up this morning you were all quiet, and now you're only nodding and shaking your head at me. It's so weird," Caio says, then immediately starts to apologize. "I don't mean *you're* weird, okay? I'm talking about the situation and the way you change, like night and day. *That's* weird, not you."

I laugh a little, because it's funny to see Caio so concerned and apologizing so much when, in fact, I *am* actually pretty weird. That's when I get an idea that might work out great, or it might be terrible. I look at the open book in my hand, and my eyes find a sentence in which the protagonist says, "That's enough! I shall take the reins of my destiny, change my life, and finally find my love."

I roll my eyes at how cliché that is, and then keep rolling

them, because that's exactly what I'm about to do: I will take the reins of my destiny and . . . you get the picture.

"I can try to explain," I say, getting up from the floor, not looking at Caio directly. "But you'll probably think I've lost my mind."

Caio seems confused but excited at the same time. I signal for him to follow me and head to the bedroom. The curtain is thin and the room is too bright. So I grab a blanket from the closet, clip two ends to the top of the window, and close the door—and in two minutes, I have a completely dark room, just as it would be if it were nighttime.

"You can lie down, if you want to," I tell Caio, and then realize that it must seem like the strangest proposition of all time.

Caio doesn't say anything. He lies down in his bed, and I lie down in mine, and we remain quiet.

I need some time to gather all the courage inside me (which is usually about zero) and think about how to approach the subject. I decide to start with the truth.

"I can't talk to you during the day because I don't like being observed. I'm embarrassed by how you might see me, and that's why I can only open up in the dark. You see? I am officially weird," I say all at once, with a little laugh at the end.

But Caio doesn't laugh.

He takes some time to process this information, and he

looks ready to get up and leave the room at any moment. I don't want him to go. I want him to be here with me.

But then he asks, "Why are you embarrassed?"

And since I have nothing else to lose, I give the truth another go.

"Because I'm fat."

It's done. The word is out. The same way things changed when Caio said, "I'm gay," things change when I say, "I'm fat." Because *fat* is the kind of word people try to hide, no matter the cost. Everyone says "chubby" or "big boned," but never "FAT." *Fat* is a word you can never take back. When you declare something, even if it's obvious to everyone already, it becomes real.

Caio takes a deep breath and, once again, seems to be choosing his words carefully. In general, that annoys me. It's really bad to be the person who always has to wait for an answer because other people are being careful with their words. I feel fragile, and I hate feeling that way.

"You shouldn't be ashamed of being who you are."

I take a deep breath so I don't say, "Easy for you to say when you're skinny, Caio." I hold back because I know he's only trying to help.

Anyone else might have advised me to lose weight. I'm so tired of listening to diet tips I never asked for or exercises I don't want to try. Caio could have acted like everyone else.

But it makes me happy to know that he's not like that.

We remain quiet for a while. My mind goes back and forth between the relief of putting it all out there and the ridiculousness of needing to hang a blanket over a window in order to tell the guy I like that I'm fat.

Luckily, my mom walks through the front door, calling my name. I run to open the bedroom door and step out of the darkness. Caio is right behind me, and we spend the rest of the afternoon pretending like nothing ever happened.

*

One thing you need to know about my mom is that she's totally obsessed with cable TV. She'll watch anything: cooking shows, documentaries about animals, bizarre reality shows, and shows about hoarders. I don't complain because I love it, too.

A while ago, she came up with themed nights, like Culinary Mondays (when the two of us would cook together), Stylish Thursdays (basically, laundry day), and Décor Saturdays (when we'd try to put all the decoration tips we'd learned into practice, using only materials that we had at home, and obviously it all turned out hideous). None of the themes lasted very long. Except Musical Wednesdays. Contrary to what the name might suggest, Musical Wednesdays are not for karaoke (which wouldn't be an awful idea). My mom discovered she loves musicals after she watched *Mamma Mia!* for the first time, and ever since, we've watched one musical every week, always on Wednesdays. Thanks to that, I've found a lot of incredible movies, and some not as incredible. (Did *The Sound of Music* really need to be three hours long?)

If you're wondering what my favorite musicals are, fear not! I have the list ready:

- *The Wizard of Oz* (1939): One of the best classics of all time. Besides the really fun songs, it has everything a good story needs: friendship, a strong lesson, and witches.

- *Les Misérables* (2012): My mom hated it, but I couldn't care less. This movie is amazing! I cried from the beginning to the end. I fell in love with all the characters who basically sing their every line. *Les Misérables* serves as proof that Hugh Jackman is the hottest man in the world, even when he's covered in mud from head to toe.

- *Seven Brides for Seven Brothers* (1954): This movie tells the story of a woman who marries a guy to escape her hard life as a cook at a bar. The guy is good-looking, and he has a nice beard and a house in the hills. When she gets to said house, she finds out that the handsome man has seven lazy brothers, and they all expect her to cook, do the dishes, and clean the house. But, of course, she doesn't! She teaches them some basic life skills (such as taking showers).

- *Dreamgirls* (2006): One word: Beyoncé.

- *Footloose* (1984; for god's sake, do *not* watch the remake!): A super-young Kevin Bacon moves to a city where, believe it or not, it's forbidden to *dance*. He breaks all the rules, everyone dances together, and in the end there's glitter rain.

We're all in the kitchen when my mom explains the dynamics of Musical Wednesdays to Caio. At first, I can't tell if he's excited or desperate.

"Since you are our guest, you get to choose tonight's movie!" she says.

He flashes a smile. "Are there any rules?"

"It has to be a musical. And it has to have a happy ending, because today I don't want to cry," my mom says, and Caio looks to be consulting his mental list of movies with happy endings.

"Can I make brigadeiro?" he asks.

"No need to ask twice!" my mom answers, handing him a pan.

Caio picked *Hairspray*—the 2007 version with John Travolta as a woman and Michelle Pfeiffer with all that Botox. Of course, I'd watched this one before. It's fun, the music is amazing, and Zac Efron looks really cute. My mom, who had never heard of *Hairspray* until tonight, was all excited. She danced in her spot on the couch, but when the last song came on, she pulled me up and we danced to "You Can't Stop the Beat" together. I was dying of embarrassment, but Caio got up, too, and the three of us danced until the credits rolled up on the screen.

It had been a while since we'd had such fun on Musical Wednesdays. And I can't believe I just used that name as if the day were something official, and not something my mom made up.

By the time the movie ends, it's already late, but I need to shower. I turn on the water and start thinking about Caio's choice of movie and our humiliating conversation in the dark this afternoon. *Hairspray* is an incredible film about the fight for civil rights during segregation. It's about conquering prejudice and opening spaces to all. It's also a film about a fat protagonist who, in the end (spoiler alert!), ends up with Zac Efron!

The part of my brain that loves to come up with unlikely theories starts whirring, and I wonder if this could be a sign.

Caio might be sending hints that he wants to be the Zac Efron of my life. Earlier today I told him I'm embarrassed to talk to him during the daytime. *Because I'm fat*, I said out loud. Then, a few hours later, he picked a movie with a lot of nice morals, one of them being *It's okay to be fat*. And that makes me feel a little happy.

When I go back to my room, properly dressed in my sleeping shorts and an old Felix the Cat T-shirt (always very sexy), Caio is already in bed. He's on the phone, talking to his mom. From what I gather, he's trying to convince her that he wasn't out in the rain in the last few days and that he doesn't see how she got the idea that he sounds like he has a cold.

He hangs up and turns off the light, and we both lie there in the dark. I feel that little flutter in my stomach because I know now is our official time to talk. I'm afraid that things between us are going to be weird, or that Caio will start suggesting different ways for me to accept my body or, worse, get thin. So, as if our weird conversation earlier hadn't happened, or as if Caio hadn't picked a Musical Wednesdays movie that *definitely* was intended to be a message for me, I start a conversation in the most casual way I know how.

"Wanna play a game?" I ask.

"What kind of game?"

"It doesn't have a name, because I made it up. But for now,

we can call it The Best and Worst in the World." I proceed to explain how we play, trying not to make it sound silly. "It works like this: One player names a category, and the other has to give both the best and the worst in the world in the category. But it's only fun if you pick very specific categories to make the other player really think. You can't say, like, fruit. Or color. Or things the other player will have a favorite and least favorite of already."

I did my best to explain, but Caio still seems confused. I don't know how to make the rules clearer because I've never had to say them out loud. It's a game I usually play by myself.

"You'll start to get it as we play. We can start with easy categories, and then make it harder."

"Okay, can I go first?" Caio says, a little disinterested. I say yes, and he gives me the first category: "Movies with aliens."

"Easy peasy," I say. "The best in the world is *E.T.*, because it has aliens, friendship, and adventure. The worst in the world is *The Invasion*, because it features Nicole Kidman in one of the worst roles of her entire career, the poor woman."

Caio laughs a little at my answer.

"Nice ones," he says. "But I think I'd pick *Space Jam* as the worst in the world, because it has aliens playing basketball against Bugs Bunny. Who thought *that* would be a good idea?"

"Basically everybody?!" I say, aggravated, because *Space Jam* is wonderful, and I feel an unreasonable need to defend it as a cinematic masterpiece. But seeing as I rarely get into arguments, I move on and change the subject by giving Caio a new category. "Girl bands with four members or fewer."

"Impossible!" He answers almost immediately. "Because the best in the world has five members, and the worst has two hundred. The Spice Girls and the Pussycat Dolls, if you were wondering."

"Doesn't matter. I want girl bands with four members or fewer. Figure it out!"

"Can I choose the Cheetah Girls? After Luciana left, there were only four," Caio says.

"The Cheetah Girls being the best or the worst?"

"Worst" is his determined answer.

"So, no, you can't choose them," I say, because I love the Cheetah Girls and also feel an unreasonable need to defend them.

"Fine. Girl bands with four members or fewer. Best in the world is Destiny's Child. Worst in the world is Little Mix."

I let out a guffaw when I'm reminded that SNZ was once a thing.

As we take turns, the categories become more complicated, but in the process I get to learn more about what Caio likes. He loves Lady Gaga, too (the category was pop divas who have starred in bad movies), and the scene in *13 Going on 30* where everyone dances to Michael Jackson's "Thriller" (the category was musical scene in movies that are not musicals).

We're both very sleepy, but we don't want to go to bed yet. The game has now reached bizarre levels, since Caio suggested the category unexpected male butts in movies. I laughed out loud, but then, surprisingly, I had my answers ready.

"Okay, here goes. Unexpected male butts in movies. Best in the world is Hugh Jackman's butt in *X-Men: Days of Future Past*. Worst in the world is Matt Damon's lanky ass in *The Martian*."

Caio lets out a sleepy laugh, but he seems surprised.

"I thought this category would have stumped you, but you answered right away!"

"Don't underestimate me, I'm an *asspecialist*." And with that, both of us go silent, taking in what I just said.

I start thinking of a way to change the subject when Caio suddenly starts laughing harder than ever. He keeps repeating *asspecialist* as if it is the funniest thing in the universe, and I start laughing as well because it seems like the right thing to do.

"You're funny, Lipé," Caio says, catching his breath.

I freeze, because no one has called me that since my grandma died. What's strange is that I thought I'd get mad if someone else, at any point in my life, called me that, but I'm not mad. I feel . . . comfortable. It feels like coming back home after traveling for weeks and realizing how much you missed your own bed.

Caio notices my silence.

"Is it okay if I call you that? Lipé, I mean. Because if you think it's too much, just tell me, and I'll—"

"It's okay," I interrupt. "I like being called Lipé."

And then I fall asleep. With a smile on my face.

DAY 7

I WAKE FROM A FUNNY DREAM. Caio and I were living in our own musical, singing one song after the other. And for no apparent reason, we were wearing Power Ranger costumes. The songs were about stupid things, like breakfast. While I was dreaming, the lyrics seemed amazing, but now that I'm awake, I realize that they were actually really bad ("Hot buns, cold milk, this is what makes me thrilled! Thri-illed!" See what I mean?).

When I open my eyes, I still have that silly smile on my face. I probably had it while I was sleeping, and if Caio saw me with it, I hope he found it funny instead of disturbing. I want to tell him about my dream—sing him the song, even. But there's a knot in my throat.

The blanket I hung on the window yesterday fell to the floor during the night, and the bedroom is flooded with light. I can see dust particles floating in the sunlight, and they mesmerize me for a few seconds. It's funny how dust is always there, but we only *really* see it when there's a beam of light. It's kind of like me, but the other way around. Because

I only show myself in the dark, you know? And also because I never go unnoticed.

Okay, that was the worst metaphor of all time. Let's move on, shall we?

When I look over, Caio is already awake, reading *The Two Towers*. He seems focused on the story, but he can see that I'm up. Without peeling his eyes away from the book, he utters the first words of the day.

"Good morning, Lipé."

"Good morning, Caio."

I only now realize how hard it is to come up with a nickname for a name like his.

Here we go again. I don't know what to say, and I feel like wrapping myself in my blanket and pretending I'm not here. I hear Olivia's voice in my head repeating itself a thousand times, reminding me that this week's challenge is to talk to this guy. I consider possible interesting subjects to start the day—"Sleep well?" "How do you like the book?" "Is it just me, or is it chilly?"—but I don't say any of that. Because I'm tired of not knowing what to say, and of feeling a ton of words stuck in my throat. I'm tired of being a speck of dust dancing in the air without ever being noticed. (All right, all right. No more dust metaphors, I promise.)

And so, to break the silence, I tell the truth. Because those who tell the truth open the path for good things to happen.

I think my mom said that once. Or maybe it was Dumbledore.

"My therapist gives me challenges sometimes—you know, tasks that I need to accomplish between sessions. And I know you didn't ask to be a part of it, but—surprise!—my challenge this week is to talk to you during the daytime, in the light. A normal conversation. No blanket hanging on the window. And I don't want it to seem as if I'm begging, like 'Caio, for god's sake, please talk to meee!'" I say all at once, and he starts laughing because I said that last part in a funny voice. "But, well . . . I basically am," I add, staring intently at the ceiling and hoping he won't think this is as ridiculous as I think it is.

"That's cool. Does she always give you a challenge? Do you get some kind of reward?" he asks, and he seems genuinely interested.

"I don't get rewards," I say, intrigued, because it has never occurred to me. I'll suggest that in our next session. "But if you can help me, I'll give you one."

A steamy, passionate kiss, I think.

"Okay, I'll help. What do I have to do?" He closes the book and sits on his bed to get a better look at me.

His gaze makes me feel anxious.

"I don't know. The conversation needs to be relevant. And last at least ten minutes. Or however long normal conversations last. And it has to be during the day. In daylight. Those are the rules," I say, still looking at the ceiling, because if my eyes see Caio in his pajamas, I might die.

"Okay. You can start talking."

I'm suddenly under pressure, and I can't get my thoughts straight. So I say the first thing that comes to mind. "I dreamed about you."

Caio muffles a laugh.

It takes me a moment to realize that this sentence can mean a million different things. I start to explain myself, trying to seem as calm as possible. I tell him about my dream—the musical, the lyrics about breakfast, and the Power Ranger costumes. He laughs out loud at that last part.

"Which Power Ranger would you be?" he asks, changing the focus completely.

I'm happy for it, because I wouldn't have known how to continue the conversation after describing that bizarre dream.

"I've never really given it much thought," I say. "I would definitely never be the red one. The red ones are always boring."

"I'd be the Pink Ranger, of course," he says, striking a funny pose, with the tip of his right foot on his left knee.

Until this very moment, I never imagined this was a real pose that human beings could strike. Never.

"Then I'd be yellow," I say, because my favorite color is

yellow. And because I don't know what else to say.

"And we would be BFFs!" He laughs and strikes another diva pose.

I laugh, but inside I feel the pressure of twenty buckets of cold water hitting me at once, because this whole "Pink and Yellow Rangers" thing reminds me that "BFFs!" is the closest I can ever be to Caio.

"Ten minutes," he says, snapping his fingers and checking his phone.

"Huh?" I'm confused.

"The ten minutes are up. Twelve, in fact. Congratulations, Mr. Felipe, you've just completed your challenge!" he announces in a voice that, as far as I can tell, is supposed to sound like Olivia's.

It becomes immediately clear that he's never gone to therapy in his life, because he thinks therapists call their patients *Mr.*

"Yeah, seems like it," I say, and decide not to correct him in this instance.

"But you don't have to go quiet again. We can keep talking."

"Yes, yes. Of course. We can. We can talk so much. The whole day. If you want to, I don't know. If it's not boring to spend an entire day just talking to me," I say, getting lost in my senseless words.

"I have an idea!" He starts texting someone on his phone. "I'm talking to Becky, and she wants to meet you! Do you want to go out today?"

"Hmm, I don't know," I say, because I really don't.

And also because I don't really know how to process the information that Becky *wants* to meet me. Nobody has ever *wanted* to meet me of their own free will. I'm usually just a consequence in people's lives. Never a choice.

"Please, let's do it! I helped you with the ten-minute conversation, and you owe me a reward!" Caio goes for a low blow, using his abandoned-puppy face on me, and I say yes.

Who could say no to Caio's abandoned-puppy face?

When I agree to go out with him and Becky, Caio jumps up to go shower.

"Thanks. Your place is great and all, but I can't take being cooped up in here the entire time," he says with a short laugh, then leaves the room.

I let out a deep breath and, as usual, start a mental list of all the things that could possibly go wrong today.

*

My mom starts jumping up and down with happiness when I tell her Caio and I are getting lunch at the mall. For real. She's literally JUMPING.

"I have two commissions for paintings that I need to finish today, and all I need is a quiet house. Take your time.

Have fun, boys!" she says, handing me her credit card and giving me a kiss on the forehead.

And she also plants one on Caio's forehead, which I find funny. It seems like she's really taking the whole "I got myself a second son" thing seriously. Today it's chilly, and I love chilly days. I'm wearing a black sweatshirt with pockets in front, which is great because as soon as we get into the elevator, Caio and I both try to press the button for the lobby at the same time. He presses it first, our hands knock into each other, and I end up hitting the button for the second floor by mistake. I have no idea what to do with my hands.

I quickly shove them both in my pockets and Caio laughs, because when I do that, my elbow hits the first-floor button. I laugh, embarrassed, and feel my face go red, and the two of us appreciate in silence this never-ending elevator ride, stopping at every floor on the way down.

We're meeting up with Becky at the mall, which, just like most things in this town, is around the corner from where I live. One of the advantages of small-town life. Everything is nearby, so you can get anywhere very quickly.

To be honest, this might be the *only* advantage of living in a small town.

The walk is only a few minutes long, but I don't want them to be filled by awkward silence. I'm determined to eliminate all awkward silences from my friendship with Caio. I ask how he and Becky know each other, more so to avoid the silence than out of curiosity. But that changes the second I see Caio's face brighten as he starts talking about his friend. At that moment, I want to hear everything he has to say.

"We've been going to the same school since fifth grade, but she's a year older, so we've never been in the same class. She once defended me from some older guys who were giving me crap between periods, and from then on, we started hanging out."

I catch myself wondering if Caio is bullied in school, too. As well as the reasons for why people would do that. And how he's handled it. I want to ask him about all that, but I don't want to interrupt the story he's telling, now more excitedly than before:

"When I was in eighth grade and Becky was in ninth, she told me to meet up with her after class somewhere far from school, because she had something serious to tell me. At the time, I was scared, y'know? I was afraid she was gonna tell me she was in love with me and ask for a kiss. Back then, I was already sure I was gay, and at the same time, I didn't want to hurt her. After school, we went to the park downtown together and sat on a secluded bench to talk. She was all shy, didn't know how to start the subject, and I started feeling anxious."

Caio is an excellent storyteller, because at this point, I'm also feeling anxious.

"Suddenly, I pulled my notebook from my backpack and then told her to write down what she wanted to say, because that way might be easier. She grabbed the notebook from my hand, pulled out a pen from her backpack, and started writing. She crossed out three things until she was satisfied with what she'd written. Then she ripped out the tiny piece of paper, folded it in half, handed it my way, and turned her back to me. I opened the note, and it said *I like girls*. And I remember that in that moment I had to hold back a shout. Then I grabbed the pen and wrote *I like boys* right underneath it and handed it back to her from over her shoulder. She read it, let out a relieved sigh, turned back to me, and said she'd always known. Becky was the first person I told I was gay, and ever since then we've been best friends. It was easier when we got to see each other every day, but, you know, she's older. She graduated last year, went to college, started dating, and barely has time for me anymore."

Caio tells the whole story very excitedly, but I sense his voice is a bit sad when he finishes it. For a second, I'm a little angry at Becky, for being the kind of person who forgets about her friends when she starts dating. I'd never be that way! Probably because I'll never start dating. Or have friends, for that matter.

But deep inside, I feel jealous of Caio and Becky's story. I wish I had a friendship like this one. I wish the first person to know I was gay had been my best friend and not my mom.

"Now I'm even more excited to meet her," I lie.

My hands break out in a cold sweat when I meet new people. My stomach churns, and now I regret saying that I was on board for this. Too late, I guess.

We're both waiting at the meeting spot (a fountain by the mall entrance that, if you look at it from a certain angle, looks like a huge penis), and I look all around me just so I won't have to face Caio. I try so hard to pay attention to literally anything else that I barely realize he starts talking to me.

"You're going to love Becky. She's awesome. And gorgeous," he says, unable to contain his excitement.

But not very punctual, I think about fifteen minutes later when we're still waiting in front of the fountain. Suddenly, Caio smiles from ear to ear. And I notice it because at this point I've given up on trying not to look at him.

"Here she comes!"

I look over my shoulder and see Becky approaching. My jaw literally drops, because she's not like anyone I imagined. I try to close my mouth quickly before anyone notices, and to mentally organize everything I'm seeing.

Well, I won't keep you in suspense. Rebeca is fat.

In the little time it takes for her to reach us, I start

thinking about a million things. It's weird how our minds are so used to the same starting points. I didn't know much about Rebeca, and yet in my mind she was thin. I imagined her thin, because it didn't occur to me at any point that she might not be.

For a second, I feel like an asshole for thinking this way, but I have no time to follow that thread. When I snap out of it, Rebeca is already hugging me, saying it's a pleasure to meet me, and revealing that Caio talks about me a lot. It's too much to absorb all at once, so I just try to smile and seem nice.

"I'm sorry I'm late, but Caio knows me. I'm always late, so I don't even know why he still arrives on time. But I'm here now," Rebeca says, lifting her arms and waving, as if she were thanking the audience after a performance.

She has dark brown skin, and her curly hair is tied in a ponytail at the very top of her head. She's wearing a pair of earrings with Darth Vader's helmet on them. Her oversized sweatshirt says BITCH, DON'T KILL MY VIBE, and her tight jeans have a galaxy pattern on them.

I immediately decide I want to *be* this girl.

"I can't even believe we're finally seeing each other," Caio says to her, and then turns to me. "Because you know, Felipe, there are *certain people* who go to college, start dating, and forget about their friends."

"So, Felipe," Rebeca tells me, leaning on my shoulder, "there are *certain people* who don't understand how hard it is to juggle college, a crappy internship, and a long-distance relationship. And that a lecture is the last thing I need right now, you know?"

I stand between them, not knowing if this is a serious argument or if they're just joking. I also don't understand why they're using me to talk to each other. So I opt to say something sensible.

"Y'all, I'm hungry."

Rebeca laughs and grabs my hand, which startles me, but I don't let go because I don't think that would be polite.

"I like you already!" she says.

Caio smiles at me as if he's proud and relieved that I got Rebeca's approval so quickly. I'm proud and relieved because Caio smiled at me and I didn't throw up.

Together, the three of us make our way to the food court and stop at a place that serves the best burgers you can find for less than ten bucks. I order a bacon cheeseburger with extra bacon (just because), Caio orders a cheeseburger with spicy mayo, and Rebeca orders a veggie burger. When the waitress is done writing down our orders and is about to leave, Caio asks her to wait. He touches my hand, and I'm surprised because I've never been touched as much as I have today in my entire life.

"Felipe, do you want to split some fries?" he asks.

I say yes without a second thought.

While we're waiting for our food, Rebeca tells Caio everything that's happened in her life in the last few months. From what I gather, the two of them haven't seen each other since Carnival in February. I listen attentively while playing with a straw to keep my hands busy.

"I still can't believe my relationship with Melissa has lasted this long, because I swore she was going to break up with me after two weeks," Rebeca tells Caio.

"Melissa is Rebeca's girlfriend," Caio explains to me. "They met during Carnival and two days later were already official."

"The thing is, she doesn't live here. She lives a few hours away, and I spent the first three months worried because she's in a huge city full of good-looking people, and I'm stuck here for at least three and a half more years," Rebeca says, this time looking at me.

"What a shitty situation." I don't know what else to say.

"But now everything is way better. We fight sometimes, because I'm an Aries and she's a Scorpio, which is the worst combination of all time. But we make it work," she says, and I just nod because I know nothing about star signs.

"Becky has always been really into astrology," Caio tells

me, and then turns to her with a challenge. "Try to guess what Felipe's sign is. I love it when you try to—"

She doesn't even wait until he's done before blurting out, "Pisces, obviously."

And I laugh, because she got it right.

"You see?" Caio slaps the table excitedly. "She always gets it right!"

"But . . . how?" I ask.

"You'd have to be a Pisces to get along with Caio the way you do—the right way. Pisces are nice. Caio is a Cancer, and you need all the patience in the world to put up with a Cancer. They're half princess and half evil witch, if you know what I mean. You have to watch your back!" she says, whispering to me as if she's sharing a secret tip.

"Hey! I'm right here," Caio says, winking at me.

I feel my face go red because I really was not expecting a wink, least of all from Caio.

Our food arrives, we eat together, and everything is delicious. Caio and I take alternate turns when going for the fries, so our hands never touch, which is unfortunate. To be honest, I don't even know what would happen if our hands bumped over the basket of fries, but I'll admit I was hoping that it would happen.

When we're done eating, we leave the food court and start walking aimlessly around the empty mall, looking at the windows of the same old stores. Caio and Rebeca go into a stationery shop, and I ask them to wait for me there because I need to go to the restroom.

I run to the nearest bathroom, duck into a stall, grab my phone, open my browser, and type, "Are Pisces and Cancer a good match?" Search.

I discover that, yes, they are, then leave the bathroom with a smile on my face.

*

As you might have guessed, there isn't much to do on a Thursday afternoon in a small-town mall. We look at the window displays, and Rebeca tells us about how her internship at a publicity agency is torture and her boss is a full-time asshole. Caio tells us stories about a teacher who used to be Rebeca's, too, and the two of them reminisce over inside jokes. I don't understand much of what they're talking about, but I'm smiling for most of it because it feels so nice to be in their company.

I'll admit that I enjoy listening to the two of them talk about school, because I don't feel like I have to participate. I can just be quiet and watch without seeming like a weirdo. Because, for the moment, my silence makes sense.

We go into a department store that's having a clearance sale, and Rebeca walks all over the place, looking for clothes and making comments like "I don't understand this collection that they're calling 'plus size' but that only goes up to size twelve" and "These pants should come with a warning that they're only good for people who were born with literally no butt."

I'm having fun with the things she says when suddenly my eyes catch a section I didn't even know existed. At the back of the store, behind the underwear section, I find a sign that says MEN'S SLEEPWEAR and walk that way.

I never go shopping for clothes. My mom usually does that for me. Now imagine my surprise when I discover there's an entire section dedicated to pajamas, and in that section, there are superhero pajamas! I feel apprehensive right away, because every time I find cool clothes, I have to deal with the immediate disappointment of not finding them in my size. But the superhero pajama industry— unlike the therapist knickknacks industry—seems much more inclusive, and the pj's come in all sizes. I search for a Green Lantern set and find it easily. (After all, it's *green*!)

I'm not a big fan of colors. I like colors *on things*, but never on me. I hold up the Green Lantern pajamas in front of me, trying to imagine myself in them, when I hear Caio calling me.

"Psst, what about this one? It'll look exactly like the drawing that you got from the boy at the community center," he says, holding a pair of Batman pajamas in front of his body.

It's all black, with the yellow bat symbol smack-dab in the middle of the top, and though I don't really like Batman, I still buy it. Never again, beige pajamas. Never again.

*

It's late afternoon when we finally leave the mall. Rebeca needs to pick up Melissa, who's coming to visit for the weekend, and Rebeca can't stop talking about it. I don't mind because I think it's cute how she talks about her girlfriend, all lovey-dovey. And I wonder how complicated it must be to live so far away from the person you love.

Before we part ways, Rebeca throws her arms around my shoulders. She's touched me so many times throughout the day that I'm not even startled by it anymore.

"I like you. You're a nice one. I want to see you again, okay?" she says, and I answer with a smile because I like her, too. She's a nice one. And I want to see her again.

And now, looking at Caio and me, she starts planning the next day.

"Melissa is dying to see you. Let's hang out tomorrow. Just give me a call."

"But—"

"No buts allowed, Caio! Your mom is out of town, and we have to make the most of it!" she says, moving her hips in a funny dance.

Caio agrees and hugs her goodbye.

I give her a wave and say, "Bye, Rebeca!"

She turns around to leave, but before she walks away, she looks at me one last time. "You can call me Becky, hottie."

And I have no reaction, because no one has ever called me *hottie* in my life.

Granted, she might have said it ironically. Or maybe she calls everyone that. Or perhaps she really does think I'm a hottie, but in a platonic way. I look down and start walking quickly so Caio won't notice my face going red for the millionth time since we left the house.

On the way home my mom texts me: I'M STARVING!!!!!!!!!! followed by four hundred food-related emojis, crying faces, and an alien that she probably included by mistake.

Caio and I stop at a Chinese restaurant (my mom's favorite) and order takeout. When we get back and she sees the restaurant bag, she thanks me desperately, as if I had saved the world. Her hair is pulled up, forming a nest on the top of her head, and there are paint splotches all over her clothes. She takes one last look at the painting she's working on (a field of red flowers and, in the middle of the flowers, some hidden human heads) and throws the brushes in a cup filled with water.

"No more work for today! Now I just want to eat orange chicken, watch whatever crap is on TV, and have fun with my two boys!" she says, bringing the food to the living room.

I walk in right behind her, trying to let go of the fact that my mom calling us "her two boys" is pretty weird. Caio makes a funny face at me, and I think he's probably thinking the same thing.

The three of us squeeze onto the couch, each holding our little takeout containers. We watch three episodes of *The Bachelorette*, a painfully bad reality show in which a single woman is stranded in a house with, like, twenty versions of the same dude, and in the end has to pick one of them. They're all mostly white, ripped, and kind of jerks, but my mom and I love this show for how ridiculous it is.

When we're done with our TV marathon, my mom slaps my leg lightly.

"Want to see what your grandma has to tell us today?" she asks with an earnest smile on her face.

Caio looks confused. And with good reason, because he knows my grandmother is dead. My mom notices the confusion on his face and starts to explain.

"Since my mother passed away, Felipe and I look for ways not to forget her. One day, Felipe got a fortune from a fortune cookie that happened to be a phrase she used to always say. And ever since then, we like to believe that she communicates with us via fortune cookie."

It's a little weird, I know. But it's become such a ritual in our home that the possibility of Caio thinking we've lost our minds doesn't even cross mine. I look at my mom, and her eyes are watery with tears.

Caio listens to the story with a smile and strokes her shoulder.

"And what did the fortune say?" he asks, looking at me.

"'The world is yours,'" I answer, a little emotionally, which always happens when I think about Grandma Thereza.

The three of us go quiet for a few seconds, but my mom gets up, grabs the three fortune cookies from the coffee table, and distributes them among us.

"It's time to see what Grandma Thereza has to tell us. Let's go, one at a time. Caio can go first, since he's the guest."

Caio opens the cookie, removes the slip of paper, and reads his fortune.

"'Fate can be a shield or a sword. It's up to you to decide.'"

The three of us start laughing, because that doesn't make any sense.

"Sometimes Grandma gets a little confused," my mom says. Then she opens her cookie, takes out the slip of paper, and reads, "'The bird doesn't sing for a reason. It sings for a song.'"

The three of us say, "Aww," because it is a cute fortune. Then Caio and my mom turn to me, waiting for me to read mine. This is always an important moment to me, even though I know that most of the time the sentences in these cookies seem like they were pulled from a tacky Facebook page. I open my cookie, look down at the slip of paper, take a deep breath, and read out loud:

"'Amazing things might happen if you just begin to talk.'"

I swallow hard when I'm done reading, because if my grandmother is really communicating with me via fortune cookie, she could at least try to be a little more subtle, am I right?

When it's finally bedtime, I'm excited to wear my new pajamas. I mean, *really* excited. I can't remember the last time I felt this way over a new item of clothing.

I shower, put on the pajamas, and look in the mirror. Unfortunately, it's not like Anne Hathaway in *The Princess Diaries*, where she lived her entire life feeling awkward and ugly and suddenly discovers she was pretty the whole time. I'd need a lot more than new pj's for that to happen to me. But when I see my reflection, despite seeing the same old me wearing a Batman outfit, I feel better. Not *good-looking*. But better.

I leave the bathroom, and when I enter my room, I find Caio sitting on his mattress, looking as if he just had an argument. He's staring at his phone, his eyebrows scrunched together, his face red with anger, and if I listen carefully, I think I can hear him growling a little. He sees me walk in and forces a smile.

"The new pj's are cool. Look! Up in the sky! It's a bird! It's a plane!" he says.

"That's Superman," I answer.

"I'm sorry. I don't know much about superheroes," Caio says, wiping a tear from his face.

"What happened?" I ask, changing the subject completely because A) the Batman vs. Superman conversation wasn't gonna go anywhere, and B) apparently the poor guy has been crying.

"I had a fight with my mom. Again."

I let out a long breath, trying to come up with the right thing to say. I close the door, turn off the lights, and lie down on my side, seeing Caio in the light filtering through the window.

"Do you want to talk about it? I don't know what to say most of the time, but I'm good at listening."

"Today at the mall I took a photo with Becky and posted it on Instagram," says Caio.

"Right," I say, and I *actually* already knew about that. My phone sends notifications every time Caio posts something. Don't judge me, please and thank you.

"My mom saw the picture, then immediately called and scolded me so hard. She said horrible things I wish I didn't have to hear. She made it into the biggest deal—yelled at my dad, told him to cancel the rest of the trip because she wanted to come back *right away*. They won't cancel the trip, of course, but my mom loves making a scene. My dad grabbed the phone from her, said he'd deal with me, and asked me to avoid causing any more uncomfortable situations," he says, and I don't quite see where he's going with this yet.

Caio clears his throat and still his voice is a little teary when he continues the story.

"My mom doesn't like Becky. Because she's a lesbian. She thinks Becky is a bad influence, and that her mission is to drag me with her toward damnation, or something. Of course, my mom has never said any of this out loud, but I know because I'm not stupid. And I just wish she knew that, without Becky in my life, things could be much worse. I'd be much more miserable than I am already."

This information catches me by surprise. Because never, under any circumstances, have I ever imagined the remote possibility of Caio being unhappy. He's always smiling, always good-humored, and, let's be honest, freaking gorgeous.

"What makes you unhappy?" I ask, because I really want to know.

"School is hell," he answers, and for a second it feels like we're the same person. "Becky has always been my best friend. Best and only. The other kids at school started picking on me from day one. Because of my voice and the way I talk. Because I don't play soccer and don't talk to other guys. I've always faced it in silence. The teasing, the jokes, the shoves in the hallway. I even kept to myself when they wrote *Caio sucks dick* in the boys' bathroom," he says, his voice shaking as if he still needs a bit more crying.

"And you never told anyone?" I ask.

"Just Becky. She's always known about everything and always had my back. She'd stand up for me when she could, and I felt safe. But the thing is, she graduated last year, and this year I'm on my own. I know there are only six months left to go, but I can't stand it anymore. And then there's my mom, scolding me over the one person who's ever . . . taken . . . my side . . . this whole . . ." He doesn't finish his sentence because he starts crying.

And the sound of his crying breaks my heart into a thousand pieces.

I wish I could force the words out of my mouth to say something reassuring. Say that I can't take it anymore, either. Tell him I understand his pain.

I'm not sure I *completely* understand his pain, because I've never been a victim of homophobia. Being gay is something that's inside me, and when people look at me, they don't go beyond my appearance. But I *do* know what it's like to spend five hours surrounded by people who hate you. And I've come across disgusting nicknames written on my desk a bunch of times. So I guess, in the end, I actually do understand his pain.

I feel like hugging him, but I don't. Maybe I would if we were both standing, but how do you hug someone who's lying down? Without making it a super-intimate thing, I mean.

So I place my hand on his shoulder and don't say anything. And that seems to be enough because, little by little, he stops crying.

"I'm sorry for making a scene," he says, embarrassed.

"No need to apologize."

"Thanks for listening."

And then he turns to the side to try and get some sleep. My hand is still on his shoulder, and I leave it there until my arm starts going numb.

"It's going to be okay," I whisper, but I think he's already asleep.

DAY 8

ONE OF THE THINGS I hate the most about polite society is when someone who doesn't even know you starts a conversation about the weather. *Pretty chilly out there, eh? Looks like rain's coming, doesn't it? Good lord, it's a scorcher.*

But right now, I need to be that awful kind of person. Because I can't ignore the fact that yesterday I went to bed chilly, and today I woke up in hell, it's so hot. The sunlight pokes through the window early in the morning, burning my face, and there's no way I'm going to fall back to sleep.

When I wake up, Caio isn't in the bedroom anymore. I get out of bed with all the excitement of someone who's just woken up in a pizza oven, and when I get to the living room, I find Caio and my mom slouched on the flowered couch, each holding a glass of lemonade. The ceiling fan spins lazily overheard, not making a difference.

"Good lord, it's a scorcher," my mom says.

I let out a lazy moan because it's the best I can do in this situation.

The morning news is on the TV, and a reporter shows

126

data about how today might be one of the hottest winter days in our state since 1996. I grab a glass of lemonade in the kitchen, and when I come back to the living room, I end up sitting on the floor because it seems cool-ish. And also because it's impossible to sit on the couch without touching both Caio and my mom at the same time. Mixing my sweat with theirs doesn't seem like the best idea. The ice I put in my lemonade melts in two seconds.

For a few moments, the three of us are silently focused on the TV, letting out the occasional sigh. The news anchor introduces a segment about what to do with your children during the school break, and the suggestions are the same as always. Summer camps, movie theaters, public pools. But my heart stops beating during that last part. Because the TV shows a group of kids getting all wet and having a good time. And Caio's face opens up with a huge smile, like someone who's just had the best idea ever. And I feel my sweat drip down harder, because I know exactly what he's about to say.

"Wanna go to the pool?" he says.

Actually, he *shouts* it.

My mom chokes on her lemonade, because she knows me well. She knows there's nothing in the universe that can drag me to the pool. But for a second she seems to forget about that and completely ignores my freedom to make my own decisions.

"Sorry, Caio, I have a lot of work piled up. Can't even

think about having fun. But the two of you are on vacation, so go enjoy your day!"

And after dropping that bomb, she gives me two taps on the shoulder, gets up, and walks to the kitchen.

Caio gets up as well.

And I end up standing, too, because it makes no sense to sit by myself on the living room floor. But, considering that the alternative is going to the pool, I wouldn't mind just staying on the floor.

Caio's level of excitement is comparable to my level of despair. He dashes into the kitchen (and I follow because I want more lemonade).

"Can I invite my friends?" Caio asks my mom, almost jumping up and down with excitement.

"Which friends?" my mom asks, but with curiosity, not suspicion.

"Becky—Felipe met her yesterday—and her girlfriend, Melissa. I hope that's okay. I mean—"

"Lesbians?!" my mom yells in a terrified voice, feigning surprise. And then laughs out loud. "No problem at all. You know, I was almost a lesbian myself for a while in college."

Caio and I go silent, absorbing this information, and then he runs out to grab his phone, leaving my mom and me alone in the kitchen. I muster all the irony I have inside me and condense it into two words:

"Thanks, Mom."

She kisses my forehead (in the way she always does, but in this case I see it as an act of true love, since, in case you forgot, I have been sweating nonstop this entire time). Then she says, in a very soft voice only I can hear, "Son, the opportunity train only passes by once. Go enjoy your day."

I have no idea what she's talking about.

I stalk out of the kitchen in an attempt to make a dramatic scene, but it doesn't work well because my mom starts laughing at me. She might be able to make me go *to* the pool, but she can't make me go *in*.

*

About thirty minutes later, Becky and Melissa are at our place. The two of them are polar opposites. While Becky arrives totally confident, chatting nonstop and calling my mom "girlfriend" after talking to her for literally one minute, Melissa is quiet and very shy.

Her skin is very pale; her hair is long and blond and has some pink on the tips. And she might be the thinnest person I have ever seen. Her arms are bony, her legs are long, and I think whoever came up with the term *negative belly* had actually just met her.

She's a very good-looking girl. Good-looking like those models who have big eyes and gap teeth.

"Hey, my name is Felipe," I say, unsure whether I should wave, shake her hand, or go in for a hug.

I do all three at the same time, and the result is pretty clumsy.

"Nice to meet you. I'm Melissa. Or Mel. But never Meli. Please don't ever call me Meli," she says with a smile, and then I see that there's definitely a gap between her front teeth.

Officially a model.

Caio and Becky won't stop talking for one second, my mom offers the girls some lemonade, and it feels like there's a party in our living room.

While we waited for Becky and Melissa, Caio put on shorts and a tank top and applied sunscreen. I put on shorts, a T-shirt, and a Pokémon hat I got when I was a kid that surprisingly still fits my head.

I never wear tank tops. I don't like showing my arms in public. I feel as if I were attacked by two hippos, one from each side, and that they're still hanging from my arms, swinging from side to side when I walk.

(My arms are the hippos, in case you find this image hard to re-create in your head.)

I get a bag and shove sunscreen, a water bottle, three comic books, and a novel in there. My plan is basically to sit and read my stuff and answer, "In a sec!" every time someone asks me when I'm going to get in the water.

It's not the most ingenious plan, but trust me, it tends to

work. As a last resort, I can pretend that I need to go to the bathroom or run out screaming, "THIS IS A FREE COUNTRY AND NO ONE CAN MAKE ME!" if things start to go south.

"Are you all well protected?" my mom asks.

"Yes," the four of us respond at once, like the audience of a game show.

"Now let's get out of here. I'm ready to dive until my toes turn into prunes," Becky says, and I find it equal parts hilarious and gross.

*

All the kids in the building are out of school, and it's the first sunny day in months. The pool is obviously crowded. There are people running everywhere, boys and girls diving and splashing around, and endless screaming matches. I regret not having packed earbuds, too.

The pool area is surrounded by tables with umbrellas, chaise longues, and plastic chairs. We grab the last remaining vacant table and, one by one, place our junk on top of it. Becky is wearing one of those beach dresses that aren't really dresses. (I don't know what the official name is, but you know what I mean.) In a quick flourish, she sweeps it off and is suddenly wearing nothing but her bikini.

I hear a muffled laugh coming from a nearby table where one of my neighbors is sitting, wearing a big hat on her head and tanning lotion all over her body. She makes a comment I can't quite hear, but another woman responds without even trying to be discreet.

"Some people really don't have any sense, do they?"

Then the two of them share some more high-pitched laughter.

It pisses me the fuck off, because I'm an expert in laughter and mean remarks. They're talking about Becky. Who's fat. And wearing a bikini.

I want to punch my neighbors and hug Becky at the same time, but it doesn't seem to faze her.

"Good thing my body isn't here to please anyone else, *isn't it?*" she says in a much louder voice than necessary. The whole complex must hear her, and I think that's just great.

Then Becky walks toward the water as if she's strutting down a catwalk and makes a perfect dive into the pool, like a mermaid. I'm relieved that she didn't take offense to my neighbor's comment. Proud that she killed it with her dive. And embarrassed because I would never have the guts to do the same.

"You're not coming?" Caio asks, bringing me back from my imaginary scene in which I award Becky a ten out of ten for her dive.

And when I look to the side, I almost have a meltdown.

Forget everything I said about Caio in his pajamas, because now things have reached a different level:

Caio.

In.

His.

Speedo.

I'll try to be brief on this subject, because I don't want to make anyone uncomfortable, but I can promise that the view is pretty impressive. His tan body has all the right curves, the yellow Speedo perfectly hugging all the places they need to hug. Caio isn't totally ripped in random places like the protagonist of an adult romance novel. But everything about him is distributed in just the right way. It's hard for me to pick a favorite part, and yet, I immediately create a mental top three: thighs, shoulders, and butt.

"In a sec," I say, trying to gather some sense of composure.

Caio smiles and makes a perfect dive, too. I feel frustrated because *when did everyone learn how to dive?*

When I sit on the plastic chair and pick out a comic book from my bag, I realize Melissa didn't go in the pool, either.

"Want a comic book?" I offer, because it seems like the polite thing to do.

She shakes her head, and I try to focus on my reading, stopping every three seconds to watch Caio swim.

"You're wild about him, aren't you?" Melissa says.

"Pffff, no. We're friends" is my answer.

"That's what my ex-boyfriend used to say. We were together for almost three years."

"Boyfriend? So . . . before Becky . . . you . . . I mean . . ." I say, fumbling for words.

"The word you're looking for is *bisexual*," she answers with an ironic laugh.

I feel like an idiot, but Melissa lightens the mood by giving me a light punch on the shoulder.

"We were talking about you and Caio. Don't change the subject!" she says with a smile.

"You're not going in the pool?" I ask, desperately trying to change the subject.

"In a sec," she answers, and I know she isn't going to. Those of us who use "in a sec" as code for "never in a million years" understand each other.

To be honest, I feel like asking why she'd rather stay here and melt in this heat, when she's thin and can go in and out of the pool whenever she wants, and no one would make fun of her for it. If I were skinny, I'd just walk around everywhere being thin. But, of course, I don't ask the question, because I've already reached my daily limit of embarrassing conversations with total strangers.

"All right, give me one of those comics," she says.

I hand her the latest issue of *Wonder Woman* that I just bought.

An hour goes by.

An hour of silence between Melissa and me. An hour of Becky alternating between diving and floating. An hour of stolen glances at the phenomenon that is Caio-in-his-Speedo, taking place right before my eyes.

The sun is getting stronger, and several worried moms start dragging their children away. The pool isn't as loud anymore, and on a couple of occasions I even enjoy the heat on my legs and the back of my head.

"Hey, nerds!" Becky yells, splashing water at us.

We're close enough to the water that we can talk but far away enough not to be in her splash radius.

"When are you coming in?" Caio asks. When I look at him, he has a flamingo floatie on his head. Yeah, really. It's a kid's float toy, the kind you put around the waist. Of course, it doesn't fit around his waist, but it fits his head perfectly.

"Whose flamingo is that?" I ask, trying to change the subject (and also because I want to know whose flamingo it is).

"Some kid left it behind. I'm taking care of it temporarily. His name is Harry," Caio says.

"Potter?" I ask.

"Styles," he answers, breaking into a One Direction dance that makes me laugh.

That's when I notice Becky has become serious. She gets

out of the pool and walks up to our table. She gives Melissa a quick kiss on the lips, and I look around to see if my gossipy neighbors saw it (unfortunately not).

"Hello, deary," she says, and I crack a smile because I've never heard anyone call someone *deary* before.

The two of them start talking and I can't hear all of it because Melissa's voice is really soft. I can only gather what Becky is saying because apparently she wasn't born with the ability to whisper. The conversation goes more or less like this:

Becky:
"It's just us here; there's nothing to be ashamed of."

Melissa:
"Ssshh shhs shhsshh shhs sh."

Becky:
"I just want to enjoy the day with you."

Melissa:
"Shh shsh shhhhs sh."

Becky:
"You are the most beautiful girl in the world!"

Melissa:
"Shhhhhh."

Becky:
"I mean it, woman."

Melissa:

"Fine."

And then Melissa gets up, having been convinced to go into the water. She takes off her flip-flops but then hesitates before taking off her little beach dress. (What *are* those things called, anyway?) All of a sudden, she takes it off in one sweeping motion and starts walking toward the pool.

And then I see why she didn't want to take off her clothes.

Melissa is wearing a one-piece, but it can't cover her entire body. Her shoulders are covered in acne and scars from acne that was once there. Her ribs stick out against her swimsuit, as if the suit were covering a birdcage. And in the middle of her breasts I can see a long vertical scar.

Melissa doesn't dive into the pool like Becky and Caio did. She enters the pool slowly, using the little stairs that almost nobody ever uses, and grimaces when her body comes in contact with the cold water. Becky goes in right after her and starts swimming around Melissa until they're face-to-face. Their eyes meet, and Becky whispers an "I love you" that I can't hear from where I'm sitting, but I understand, anyway, because I've always been great at reading lips. And then I'm just grinning like a fool because this is one of the most beautiful things I've seen in the last few days.

In this moment, I've come to understand three things:

1. Even though she's thin, Melissa also feels insecure. Being thin is not a prize you win in the lottery of life that guarantees eternal happiness.

2. I've watched enough rom-coms and have attended enough therapy sessions to know that my happiness cannot depend on another person. And yet, I *still* wish I had someone to call me *deary* and convince me to come into the pool and tell me they love me in a soft voice, in a way you can only hear from up close.

3. The person I wish were calling me *deary* and saying they love me in a low voice is playing with an inflatable flamingo named Harry Styles and is probably oblivious to everything that just happened here.

Caio, Becky, and Melissa spend the entire day in the pool. My mom brings us sandwiches and juice for lunch, I get to read all my comics and the first few chapters of the novel I brought (a sci-fi about dinosaurs and robots), and when the sun starts going down I'm exhausted, even though I did a whole lot of nothing all afternoon. It must be the heat.

The three of them decide to get out of the water and go back home, and my heart is torn. Part of me is happy because

I can't stand to sit around anymore, but the other part will miss watching Caio in his Speedo. We collect our things and go back upstairs.

My mom insists on having Becky and Melissa over for dinner, but the two of them have plans for the evening and politely decline the invitation.

"We'll see you again tomorrow!" Becky tells Caio before saying goodbye, and that makes me happy.

First because I know how happy it makes Caio to spend time with his best friend. You can tell from the look on his face. He looks like a Labrador retriever on a road trip, his head sticking out the window and his tongue hanging out.

And second because, in a way, I feel like part of the group. Even when I'm just watching from far away, I feel like they see me. When Becky makes a joke, Caio looks at me to see if I'm laughing. When Caio says something silly, Becky looks at me before rolling her eyes. I feel like I belong. And it feels good.

"All right, let's find a time. Mel, how long are you staying?" Caio asks.

"Only until Sunday. Just another couple of days," she answers, and Becky's mouth curves down in a sad face.

Then the ritual of group farewells begins, as awkward and messy as expected. Becky hugs Caio and kisses his cheeks while Melissa does the same with my mom, then they go on, Melissa with Caio and Becky with me, and suddenly Becky is hugging Caio again and saying, "Oops, I've already said good-bye to you," and everyone is lost and talking over one another.

Melissa takes this opportunity to give me a strong hug (stronger than what's typically expected when hugging someone you've known for less than a day). Then she whispers in a very low voice to my ear, "Don't be silly; he's wild about you, too."

And I let out a nervous laugh, as if to say, "What are you *talking* about, girl?" But Melissa just smiles at me and takes off down the hallway, holding hands with Rebeca. They are so different from each other, but when they're together like this, walking in the same pace, they seem like the coolest pair in the whole world.

*

When night comes, I put on my Batman pajamas again and feel two questions thrumming in my head:

1. What the heck was Melissa talking about? I know she meant Caio. I'm not a moron. But where did she get the idea that he's into me? I wonder if it's real, official intel or if Mel is a sensitive person who can infer people's intentions. Because if it's the latter, she's wrong.

2. How many times can I wear the same pajamas without washing them? They're not like

regular clothes that you wear throughout the day, but still they stay on your body for hours. And it was hot last night. But I checked and they don't smell bad. They still smell brand-new, actually. Is it customary to own two pairs so you can wear one while the other is in the laundry? Because if that's the case, I could get myself a Robin version. Which isn't a bad idea, anyway.

When I get to my room, Caio is already in his bed, reading *The Two Towers*. That's when I notice he looks even better after a day in the sun. His skin is even tanner now, and his lips are rosier. I feel like throwing myself on top of him and asking my first question.

But since I can't really ask, "Is it true what Melissa said, that you're wild about me?" I ask question number two.

"How many sets of pajamas do you think the average person owns?"

Caio laughs and closes his book, putting a bookmark on the page he was reading.

"I own three," he answers.

"I own one," I say, hoping he's forgotten about the beige pj's.

And since I don't know what else to say, I turn off the lights and lie in bed, feeling my back hurt a little from all the sun.

"Pj's are like our best friends," Caio says. "They need to make us feel comfortable. And you don't need a bunch."

"Nice metaphor. How many best friends do you have?" I ask, and it takes Caio two seconds to answer, as if he was going through his list of best friends in his mind.

"I think just Becky. Melissa is cool, but I don't know her very well. I can't call her a good friend. I had more friends at school at one point, but they started drifting away as it became more obvious that I was . . . gay," he says the last word in a lower tone of voice, as if it were still a secret. "What about you? Who are your best friends?"

I should have anticipated Caio would ask the question back, but I'm caught by surprise. I don't have a best friend. Even when I was a kid and didn't have all the issues I have today, I didn't have a best friend. Classmates, maybe. Some cousins who would come to visit once in a while. But never a friend who would listen to all I had to say.

Caio is the first one to do that.

But *of course* I'm not about to say, "You, Caio. You are my best friend," because I don't want to sound desperate. I also can't say, "Friends? I have none," because that would be even worse. So I do what anyone else in my situation would.

"My best friend moved to Canada last year. For school. We still talk, but not as much," I lie.

"That's sad. What's his name?" Caio asks.

"Jake." I blurt out the first name that comes to mind, which, by the way, is the *worst* name I could have picked.

"A Brazilian Jake? That's fun!" says Caio, and I can hear the suspicion in his voice.

"His mom is American. He was born in Michigan and moved here when he was three. His family is always moving around because his dad sells . . . airplanes," I say.

"Oh, I see," says Caio in the voice of someone who has just heard the most unabashed lie in history.

"Jake doesn't exist," I admit with a sigh.

Caio laughs and I feel like an idiot.

"Lipé, it's fine," he says. "We can be each other's best friends. That way, you don't have to lie when people ask."

After hearing something like that, I'd normally go into a never-ending spiral about how Caio wants to be my *friend* and tweet something about being *friend-zoned* or something. But today there's no crisis. Because that was exactly what I needed to hear.

But since I'm addicted to bringing myself down, I don't miss this chance. "I've never been anyone's best friend, so I might not be the right guy for the job."

"You're doing great," Caio says. "Sitting around under the sun the whole day so I can go to the pool when you'd rather be anywhere else? That's a best-friend move."

"I'm sorry I didn't go in the water."

"Thanks for being there, anyway."

DAY 9

WHEN YOU'RE ON VACATION, every day is a Saturday. But when I wake up to the sweet smell of cake, I realize it's *officially* Saturday.

"I baked the cake a little earlier today," my mom says when I get to the kitchen.

The table is half-set. On one side, I can see a checkered tablecloth, a freshly baked orange cake, coffee, and milk. On the other, my mom's painting supplies, messy as ever.

"Where did Caio go?" I ask, trying to sound casual. When I left the bedroom, his bed was already empty.

"He went out. He's in the hallway, outside. His mom called, and I think he was embarrassed to talk to her in front of me," my mom says while serving me a slice of cake and a glass of milk.

"His mom is a lot," I say in a whisper.

"All moms are, Felipe. It's in our genes. It's hard not to be after a human being pops out of your body," she says, and it makes me laugh.

My mouth is full, and I spit out some cake crumbs by

accident. Right then, Caio walks in, breath ragged, trying to keep his calm.

"My mom is *unbearable*," he says.

I give my mom my best "I told you so" look.

"What happened this time?" I ask, my mouth still full of cake.

"She's still going on about Becky," Caio says, pouring himself a cup of coffee.

"What about her?" my mom asks curiously.

"My mom hates Becky."

"But she's such a good egg," my mom says. *Good egg* is her favorite description.

"It's because she's a lesbian," I explain, since I know it makes Caio uncomfortable to talk about lesbians in front of my mom.

My mom rolls her eyes so hard that it surprises me. I know how much she hates bigots, but I also know that she wouldn't say or do anything to offend Caio's mom.

"One day she'll come around, I'm sure," she says, placing a hand on Caio's shoulder.

"I hope so, Ms. Rita."

"For god's sake, no calling me Ms. Just Rita is fine."

"Just Rita sounds so serious," he says.

"I think it's cute when the kids at the community center call you Ms. Rita," I interject.

My mom cracks a smile. "I like Ms. Rita."

"Soooo, Ms. Rita," says Caio, making his words longer than necessary. "Tonight we're seeing Becky again, and if my mom asks, would you mind telling her you don't know anything about it?"

My mom looks up at the ceiling, considering what to say. "Let's pretend that I really don't know any of it, okay? You two can go out, come back whenever you want, but I *beg* you, Caio, please don't die in an accident. And don't get any tattoos. And don't lose any visible limbs. I don't want to have to explain any of that to your mother later."

"You got it," Caio say, kissing her on the cheek gratefully. "I just can't make any promises about the tattoo."

"If it's in a place she can't see, then it's fine." She winks.

And I get up from the table because this is the most embarrassing conversation I've ever witnessed in my life.

✻

We always get everything late in my town. Japanese restaurants weren't a thing until just last year. The first *Avengers* movie only premiered in our movie theaters in 2015. So I'm not at all surprised when Caio tells me we're going to a Festa Junina. If you're not familiar, Festa Junina is a nationwide tradition in Brazil that celebrates the harvest. There are parties and festivals all throughout the month of June, and everyone dresses up in country-style costumes and eats all kinds of delicious food.

Since the month of June went by without any festivities, they've decided to seize the opportunity and have the traditional June Festival in July. Regardless of the month, parties here are always the same. A live forró band plays in the town's main square, surrounded by food and drink stalls.

Usually these parties are pretty bad, but every year I stop by to eat some hot dogs and corn on the cob. I'll suffer through any event that features hot dogs and corn on the cob.

When it's almost dark, Caio starts getting ready to go to the festival. I'm lying in bed watching serious YouTube videos (Korean twins dancing to Madonna songs), when I see Caio pacing back and forth, removing several items of clothing from his suitcase, and trying to decide what to wear. From the face he's making, it looks more like he's choosing which wire to cut in order to successfully deactivate a time bomb.

Nearly an hour later, he's ready. I've never seen him so dressed up. His hair is up, in a cool style. He's wearing tight jeans that make his legs look so—I'm sorry but I couldn't come up with a better description—delicious, and a blue shirt with the top two buttons open.

I, on the other hand, pick my usual jeans and a black T-shirt. I go into the bathroom to get dressed, and I'm ready in two minutes. When I come back to the bedroom, Caio looks me up and down, and in his eyes I can read the word *DISASTER*.

He pauses for a second, hand on his chin, does a little more thinking, and then starts going through a pile of my clothes that's plopped on my desk chair. From the bottom of the pile he pulls out the checkered shirt that my mom bought me. The one he picked.

"I think this one would look nice," he says, handing it to me.

I put it on over the black T-shirt and start buttoning it, hoping it won't be too tight around my neck. When I get to the third button, Caio slaps my hand.

"No! It looks better open."

But when he says "looks better," I don't know if he means me or the shirt.

He grabs the sleeves and folds them carefully up to my elbow. Then he pulls my wavy hair up and hits it with a little bit of hair spray. I stand completely still and hold back a sneeze because the spray smells like a grandma. Not like *my* grandma. My grandma smelled better than this. This has more of a general grandma smell.

When Caio is done working his magic, I open my closet and look at my reflection in the big mirror inside the door. My whole life I've avoided mirrors because I didn't really like what they had to show me, but today is different. Because I look at my reflection and don't hate myself right away. Actually, for a few seconds, I even kind of like looking at it.

My hair is styled in a different way, the shirt looks nice on me (maybe red *is* my color after all), and I don't feel awful.

To be honest.

I even feel.

Handsome.

"Why didn't you ever tell me you had a mirror hidden in there? This whole time I've been using the bathroom mirror to get ready!" says Caio, bringing me back from my trance.

"Caio, this is Mirror. Mirror, meet Caio," I say, introducing the two, and Caio laughs as he gives my shoulder a little push.

In the living room, my mom is watching an episode of *I Didn't Know I Was Pregnant* (a reality show about women who, well, didn't know they were pregnant).

"WHOA!" she says when she looks up from the TV. "Where are you off to looking that good?"

Honestly, I need to rethink my wardrobe strategy, because all it took was one new shirt and some hair spray and my mom is *enraptured*.

"The June Festival in the town square," I say, my face completely red, but trying to act normal.

My mom shoves her hand in her pocket and takes out some crumpled bills. "Here's some money for corn. Have fun, and if you come home late, try not to bang the door the way you usually do. You sound like a hurricane!"

"Okay, I'll try."

"And you"—she points at Caio—"no illegal tattoos!"

The two of them laugh, my mom kisses our foreheads, and then we're off into the night. Or whatever it is you say when you're on your way to eat corn on the cob in the town square.

*

Rebeca and Melissa are already there when we arrive. The two of them are waiting for us at a plastic table by a street barbecue booth. Becky is wearing a yellow plaid shirt with a knot tied in the front, and Melissa is wearing a print dress and cowboy boots, and her hair is up in pigtails. The two of them really took the country theme to the next level.

"For once in your life you're not late!" Caio says, and the two of us take the empty seats at the table.

"For these parties it's always best to get here before the square gets too crowded with insufferable drunks," Becky answers, rolling her eyes.

The party isn't packed yet, but a few food booths already have lines. I look around and see a forró band doing a sound check on a makeshift stage, and I spot a few familiar faces, too. People from school know I exist, but I don't feel the need to say hi to them.

When I turn my attention back to the table, I notice a beer can in front of me. I don't know at what point Caio, Becky, and Mel started drinking (and I have no idea where this beer came from), but the three of them are holding up their cans and looking at me.

"A toast!" Becky says, nodding at my can.

"Ah, yes," I say, picking up the can and trying to act naturally—to not make it obvious that I've never had beer in my life.

"To festivals in the square that are kind of meh, but I love them, anyway!" Becky announces, raising her can.

"To forró bands that play the same four songs the whole night!" Caio adds, touching his can to Becky's.

"To my hair, which looks beautiful but will, in a few seconds, stink like barbecue smoke," Melissa cheers, shaking her ponytails.

"To corn on the cob, the best thing at this festival," I say timidly, but it makes me happy when the three of them laugh.

Caio takes a gulp of his beer, then I take a deep breath and do the same.

I'm not gonna lie, it's pretty bad. Bitter and strong, and it must not be my lucky day, because mine is warm. I grimace so hard that Becky notices right away.

"You've never drank before, have you?" she asks.

I shake my head.

"I swear it tastes better with time, and not all of them are warm like this. Warm beer tastes like piss."

I shrug as if I don't care and keep sipping little by little.

The band starts to play and we have to raise our voices to hear one another. We spend some time listening to Mel and Becky talking about their relationship. Mel's grandparents live in town, so she uses that as an excuse to come see Becky. They say weekends are always too short, but love trumps distance. I smile when they say that, but deep down I find it a little cliché.

"How did you two meet?" I ask them.

"I love that story! Tell him, tell him!" Caio says excitedly, poking Becky's arm.

"It was Carnival, and fate brought Melissa to town—" says Becky.

"Fate, in this case, being my grandparents' anniversary," Melissa interrupts.

"I prefer to call it fate," says Becky. "Long story short: Caio and I came to a street party in this very square. It was seven o'clock, and his mom was already calling him desperately, telling him to come home, and Caio, always the softy, just left. Totally abandoned me here, by myself, at the most depressing street party of all time."

"Draaaama," Caio says softly, in a high pitch.

"Then I stumbled upon her," Becky says, wrapping Melissa in her arms. "Literally."

"I had lost one of my contacts," Mel says. "I knelt down, certain that I could find it. Becky apologized a thousand times for bumping into me. I said it was fine, but that I had to find my contact. And you know what she said to me?"

"'You'll never find it. You can stop looking now and kiss me instead,'" Becky answers right away.

I laugh out loud. "And did you?"

"I stared at Becky from up close because I couldn't see very well," Mel continues. "Then I covered my left eye to try and get a better look and she said, 'I know you can't see very well, but I swear I'm pretty.' So I kissed her."

"And it was the best kiss in the world. I'd have kissed her forever, but after a few minutes someone threw a beer can at my head because this shitty town would rather see a public hanging than two girls kissing," Becky says. "And speaking of beer . . ." She gets up and doesn't finish the sentence.

And I know she went to get more.

That's when I realize that, as I was listening to their story, I finished my can. At some point, the beer went from being really bad to acceptable.

"Now I want to hear *your* kissing stories," Mel says to Caio and me, propping her elbows on the table as if she is getting ready for a long and captivating tale.

The question throws me off, and my thought process goes more or less in this order:

- She wants to hear the story of how Caio and I kissed?

- Probably not, as we never have.

- Which is a shame.

- So she wants a *general* kiss story, is that right?

- Which is still kind of panic inducing, considering I've never kissed anyone.

Before I can think of how to get myself out of the situation (grabbing some corn on the cob on the way), Becky comes back with more beer, and Caio is already talking.

"So, I have a kiss story. But it's not a beautiful one like yours. It's kind of depressing, actually," he says, a little embarrassed.

"I love depressing stories!" says Mel, with an exaggerated expression that I can't tell if it's genuine or a joke.

"Last year, Becky and I went to the next town over, to an *alternative* club," Caio starts, but he's soon interrupted by his best friend.

"Worst. Club. Ever," she says. "We had to dupe Caio's parents and get fake IDs that in the end we didn't even need, and the DJ only played David Guetta."

"And that wasn't even the worst part!" Caio adds, trying to hold back a laugh. "When I realized the party was going to be a disaster, I decided I was going to kiss the first person who showed any interest in me. I ended up kissing this boy named Denis. He was kind of cute, actually . . ."

"He was *not*," Becky interrupts again.

"But Denis's kiss was the worst thing I have ever experienced in this life," Caio goes on, disregarding Becky's interruption. "The big problem was, Denis liked to bite while kissing, and I don't know who came up with this idea that biting and kissing should mix, because they shouldn't. Denis was just *chewing* on my mouth for like five minutes until a Black Eyed Peas song came on, and I had to pretend I liked it. I said, '*Ohmygod*, I gotta dance 'cause this is my jaaaaam!!!' And then I went on to dodge the guy for the remainder of the night."

Becky and Mel are laughing along, and I have a tight smile on my face as I'm trying to delete the mental picture of Caio's mouth being chewed on by another guy. Whose name is Denis. Who most certainly is not fat.

"Your turn to tell us a kiss story, Felipe! Good or bad," Becky says, and the three of them stare at me.

I'm nervous and exasperated and feel like disappearing. In the background, I notice the band is playing a forró cover of Britney Spears's "Toxic," which is at the same time horrible and wonderful.

I take a deep breath and a long gulp of my beer, then tell them the first story that comes to mind.

"I have a great-aunt, Lourdes, who comes to town every

year for All Souls' Day. One time, when she came to say goodbye, I moved in for two kisses, one on each cheek, but she surprised me with that old saying, 'You need three if you want to get married!' Which doesn't make any sense whatsoever. I wasn't expecting a third kiss, so I turned my head by accident, and that's how I ended up kissing my sixty-four-year-old great-aunt on the lips," I say.

Everyone goes silent.

The next second, the three of them are guffawing. And I start laughing, too, because what else can you do after admitting to having kissed your great-aunt on the lips?

I look at the beer cans on the table, and I'm overcome with gratitude. Because if it hadn't been for the beer, I doubt this story would actually be funny.

We share stories for the rest of the night. Some are really fun (the time Caio's dad gave him his mom's Christmas present by accident, and Caio opened the box to find a red lace thong and decorative candles), while others are tragic (like when Mel had to get an emergency heart surgery right on the day of her college admission exams, so she couldn't take the test *and* ended up with a huge scar on her chest).

And we change subjects like that, from thongs to surgery, from cake recipes to internet memes, from politics to TV series. I contribute when I think I should, laugh more than I'm used to, and after the third (or fifth) beer, I can't even remember the name of the boy who kissed and/or chewed on Caio's mouth. (That's a lie, I do remember. His name was Denis.)

The booze makes me hungry, and when I look around trying to find the corn booth, my eyes meet his. Bruno. I feel the smile fade from my mouth as I stare at the guy who makes my life a living hell. Jorge appears right next to him, and Bruno points in my direction. I shouldn't have stared, but the part of my brain that tells me to look down isn't working.

When the two of them get close to the table where we're sitting, Caio is telling a story, but he's interrupted by Jorge's strong (and drunk) voice.

"Butterball! You're already here taking care of all the food at the party!" he says.

Bruno laughs a high-pitched laugh and comes closer to me.

At the same moment, I can feel my face go red with anger. Becky, Mel, and Caio look surprised, and the three of them turn to me with expressions that say, "Do you know these two?" I don't know how to wriggle out of this one.

"What? You're not gonna introduce us to your friends? Blondie here is kinda hot," Jorge says, pointing at Melissa.

Becky slams the table with her fist. It looks like she's about to lunge at him at any moment.

"Nobody wants you here. Go away, dude," Becky says in

a hard voice, then scoots closer to Mel, who's obviously embarrassed, and grabs her hand.

"Aaah, so Blondie here is a dyke?" Jorge asks, his voice dripping with scorn, and Bruno is still laughing.

That's when Jorge notices Caio at the table. He pauses for a second to watch us, and then goes back to staring at me with a confused expression.

"What the hell, Butterball! Is this your little boyfriend? You trying to tell me that you're not only fat, but now you're a fag, too?"

And then it all happens very quickly. Bruno bursts in a loud laugh and starts poking my back. Caio looks at me in desperation, and I can see his eyes filling with tears. Rebeca is pissed off and threatens to get up, but I do it first.

I don't know if it's the booze that makes me brave, or if it's the desire to defend my friends. Maybe it's just the fact that right now I *have* friends. All I know is that I get up, and for the first time, I'm facing these two without looking down. Without feeling small. In fact, I suddenly realize I'm a little taller than Jorge, and *way* taller than Bruno. And that makes me even braver.

At first, I don't know how to stand up for myself. I'm not going to lie to them. Yeah, I'm gay. And, clearly, I'm fat. Denying either of these facts isn't going to win me any arguments. So I don't think I have much choice.

"Bruno, Jorge," I say, looking the two of them in the eyes, my voice louder than I intended. "Go *fuck* yourselves."

And the two of them go quiet. Not even a little laugh from Bruno. Jorge seems confused because, for the very first time, I did something. And I'm still standing, hoping they will go the hell away, because I have no plan B.

"Calm down, man, calm down. Can't you take a little joke, Butterball?" Jorge says with a half smile on his face, as if I hadn't taken a lifetime of jokes already.

At this point, Becky punches the table again, and it startles Bruno. I hold back my laughter, because I don't want them to think everything is okay.

"Okay, then, man. We're gonna go. But I'll see you again at school," Jorge says in a menacing tone, then turns and leaves. Bruno, like the good doormat he is, follows right behind.

I collapse on my chair, taking a deep breath and trying to understand everything that just happened. I wait out my anger, taking a sip of my beer (the last one, I swear), and when I look at Caio, he's smiling at me.

"I'm sorry. I didn't mean to—" I start to say.

"You go to school with these dumbasses?" Becky interrupts.

I nod.

"Look, Fe," she starts in a calmer voice. That makes me smile; no one has ever called me *Fe*. "I had to put up with those types at my school, too, and I thought it was going to get better in college. Spoiler alert—it doesn't. The world is full of assholes and that's never going to change."

"Becky, always the optimist," Caio says, giggling.

"But it's the truth! Things will always be more complicated for those of us who don't fit their petty standards. When was the last time you had it easy?"

I stop and think for a while before I answer. "When I was eight and it was cute to be chubby."

"When I was eight, my aunts were already insisting I should go on a diet," Becky says. "When you're a girl, being fat is never cute. When you're a girl, you must always be skinny."

I swallow hard, because I've never considered that.

"Now picture this: I'm fat, a woman, and Black. Who has to walk down the street and hear all sorts of offensive comments. And then when I was about twelve, I realized I was into girls, and all the bad things I used to hear out on the streets I now had to hear at home, too. Things get even worse when folks stop talking and start *doing* things to you instead. To bring you down. To *break* you down." As Becky talks, her voice dims into a whisper.

For the first time since I met Becky, I catch a glimpse of her vulnerability. For a moment, she's not the strong, tough, and funny girl I've gotten to know in the last few days, and I feel my heart tighten in my chest. I wish I could protect this girl for the rest of her life.

"No one can protect us but ourselves," she says, as if reading my thoughts. "But, look, Felipe, I swear to you that one day things will get better. One day you'll learn to like who you are a little better, and that'll be reflected in what other people see when they look at you. There will always be assholes, but we learn to fight back. That's the most important thing—to not put your head down, to fight for the right to marry who you love, for the right to have your body respected regardless of what it looks like or what you're wearing. To fight for the right to walk down the street without being attacked for the color of your skin."

Caio, Melissa, and I listen attentively to Rebeca's speech. I'm afraid I'll blink and miss an important part. When Becky is done talking, we all sit in silence. Nobody knows what to say. I feel like clapping, but I'm not sure that would be appropriate.

"Booze always inspires me," Becky says finally.

And we all start laughing and talking at the same time. But Becky gives me a side hug and whispers in my ear, "You knocked it out of the park, Fe!"

And if I'd known that telling Bruno and Jorge to go fuck themselves would make me feel this good, I'd have done it ages ago.

*

It's past midnight when the party ends. Little by little, the food booths close down (and yes, I did get my corn on the cob in time), the band stops playing, and the square empties out.

"Will you still be around town tomorrow, Mel?" Caio asks when the four of us are making our way back home.

"Yeah, until late afternoon, more or less," she answers while smelling the tips of her hair. From her expression, they probably smell like barbecue smoke.

"Look, Caio," Becky interjects. "I know you love me, but tomorrow it's just me and her," she says with a wink.

Caio pretends to be offended and puts his arm around my shoulder.

"We don't care, do we, Lipé? Tomorrow it's also just me and him," he says, and from the sound of his voice, he's a little drunk.

I am, too, but that doesn't stop me from breaking into a cold sweat because Caio is practically hugging me. To my disappointment, the moment only lasts three seconds. Caio lets go of me, almost tripping in the process, and then jumps on Becky to say goodbye.

"Don't you dare go forgetting I exist, you hear me?" he says, his face shoved against his friend's neck.

"I never do," Becky responds.

We say goodbye to the girls and make our way home. I'm

surprised when Caio puts his arm around my shoulders. I'm a few inches taller, so he has to walk on the tips of his toes.

All of a sudden, I feel brave again. I can feel the adrenaline running through my body from the top down. I take a deep breath, raise my arm, and let it fall around Caio's shoulders, too. We're hugging each other now.

We need to stop walking because, for a moment there, we're a tangle of arms, and even walking is challenging in this position. But he won't remove his arm, and I won't, either.

Caio looks me directly in the eye and stomps his right foot on the ground, and I immediately understand what he wants to do. We go the rest of the way in coordinated steps.

Left.

Right.

Left.

Right.

*

When we get home, I do my best to heed my mother's orders. I try to open the front door quietly and, as expected, fail. Caio whispers something I don't understand, and I burst into quiet laughter for no reason.

After a few frustrated attempts at getting the key into the right hole, I manage to lock the door and head to the bedroom while holding Caio straight, since he's trying to bump into every wall in the house. I throw myself on the bed, and Caio stands in the doorframe.

"I need water," he says in a low voice.

And before I can say anything, he starts ambling down the hall. When my head touches the pillow, the world begins to sway. I try to find the lonely star on the ceiling, but the booze multiplies it into multiples. An entire constellation in my own room.

"I brought you some," Caio says, coming in and closing the door behind him. He seems a little more sober, but when he takes a step forward to hand me the glass, he trips on a shoe that is lying on the floor, falls on his knees on his mattress, and spills the entire glass of water all over it.

The mattress softens the landing, which is great because the last thing I'd like to deal with now would be a hurt Caio. Or a broken glass.

"Is everything okay?" I whisper.

And Caio starts laughing.

This laughter is different from all the laughter I've ever heard coming from his mouth. The last few days have made me an expert in Caio's laughter, and this is a first. It's high-pitched but controlled. He's trying to be quiet, but at the same time needs to let it out. When he tries to catch his breath, he grunts like a pig, exactly like Sandra Bullock in *Miss Congeniality*, and that gets me, too. I shove my face into my pillow and laugh until my belly hurts. In a situation not involving three or five cans of beer, this wouldn't be that funny.

Suddenly, my face still against the pillow, I can feel a presence. I snap my head up, startled, and find Caio squeezed at the end of my bed. I'm not very good with numbers, but I believe 40 percent of his body is touching mine as he shoves me against the wall in his attempt to conquer more mattress space.

I go quiet. My head, which just a minute ago wouldn't stop spinning, is now aware and alert. It's as if I'd pushed a button that removed all the alcohol from my body in one second.

Satisfied with the space he took over, Caio turns to face me. His breath is heavy, and I can smell the alcohol on it. His eyes are wide open, but each blink lasts some time, as if he is fighting sleep. His hair is plastered against his sweaty forehead, and almost all his shirt buttons are undone.

"I'm not sleeping on that wet mattress," he says, his face so close to mine that I can't even see his mouth. All I can see are his eyes.

Caio lets out another piglike laugh. But this time I don't laugh along.

"It . . . it's okay. Y-you can have my bed. I'll go down there," I stammer.

I try to get off the bed (which is really hard when your head feels like it weighs about two tons), but Caio is quicker. He pushes my shoulders down, making me lie back in bed.

"No," he says. "Stay here with me."

And I do.

Caio leans his head against my shoulder and closes his eyes. I lie there, looking at the ceiling, not quite understanding what's happening. I feel his chest go up and down in heavy breaths. I feel my heart hammering in my chest as if a band were marching through it.

My arm starts to go numb, but I don't want to move. Because I don't want this moment to end. So I close my eyes and think about how nice it would be to sleep like this every day, and suddenly I'm already asleep.

DAY 10

I WAKE UP EARLY AND it takes me a while to understand all that's happening. My back hurts, my clothes are drenched in sweat, and my breath tastes like a mix of beer and corn. My head itches, and when I try to raise my hand to scratch it, I notice that my arm is stuck. Under Caio. Who's still asleep. In my bed, in case that part was unclear.

You know all the things I said about Caio being a gorgeous sleeper? I guess they don't apply when he spent the night before drinking. Caio's mouth is open, and he's snoring loudly, leaving a streak of saliva on my sleeve. Surprisingly, I'm not grossed out by it.

As carefully as I can, I pull my arm out slowly, holding his head so the movement won't frighten him. I drag myself to the end of the bed, trying not to be loud, and stand up.

And that's when the pain hits me.

I feel it in my eyes first, then it moves up through my head before looping around to the back of my neck. I feel a throbbing pain as if a gong were going off inside my head.

I check the digital watch on my nightstand. It's not even

eight o'clock yet. I walk toward the kitchen, prepared to take anything from the cupboard that will make this headache go away. I walk down the hall quietly, but as soon as I get there, I realize my discretion was pointless. My mom is awake, painting in silence.

"Sit down," she says, not looking at me.

I sit on the chair in front of me. On the table I find a glass of water and aspirin.

"Hnnhn" is my attempt at saying "good morning."

My mom puts her brush in a glass of water, cleans her hands on the hem of her shirt—which is already smudged with paint—and sits down across from me. With a grave expression on her face, she pushes the water and the pills toward me, and I take them. The feeling of water running down my throat already makes me feel considerably better.

"Look, Felipe. I don't want to turn this into a lecture about drinking," she says.

"What do you mean?" I try to play stupid because I can't think of anything better.

"I know you've been drinking. From the moment you got here, from the two hundred tries it took you to unlock the door, from the way your clothes smell. I know."

Her expression is the gravest I've ever seen. Of course, my mom and I have had fights before, but she's never used this tone with me. As if the subject is of the utmost importance. I want to apologize, to explain that it was just a couple of beers, that it honestly doesn't even taste that good, but I don't say any of that.

"You're about to turn eighteen. You'll make your own decisions, go on with your life, and I think I've taught you everything I needed to at this point. But yesterday, for the first time ever, I felt unsure about you. I spent the night tossing and turning, wondering if I'm a good mother or—"

"Of *course* you are!" I interrupt, because I can't sit here and listen to my mother say something this absurd.

"Pssst, quiet. I'm speaking," she says, bringing a finger to her lips. "Like I said, this is not a lecture about drinking. I feel like I can trust you to be responsible. Even if you couldn't cover your tracks from last night!"

"I couldn't?" I ask, genuinely confused, trying to remember if there's a chance I threw up in the bathroom.

My mom has only to point at me, and I get it. I don't need a mirror to know that I look a mess.

"What I am afraid of," my mom goes on, "are the things you are able to hide. The things you *don't* tell me."

"You can rest assured, Mom. Those are things I tell to the therapist."

She lets out a soft chuckle and holds my hand.

"I wish I could know everything that goes on in your head," she says. And after a moment she continues, "Well,

169

almost everything. I wish I could help you get through all the crises of this time in your life so you won't get hurt. I know sometimes we feel like we can take on the world after we've had two cans of beer."

Or five, I think.

"But you will always be my boy. And I will always be your mom. So you can count on me, always. Don't hide things from me, son. You can tell me about what's happening in your life. Because I love you and nothing will ever change that."

I don't understand what she's expecting from me in this moment. I don't understand if she wants me to apologize, if she wants me to tell her everything that happened last night, or if she wants to know everything that happened in the rest of my life.

Regardless of her expectations, my head still hurts and I'm in no condition to come up with anything smart to say.

"I need your help, then," I say, and there's a spark in her eyes at the possibility of me opening up to her. "How do I make this headache go away?"

She laughs halfheartedly, unable to hide her frustration.

"It's called a hangover, Felipe," she says, getting up and slapping the back of my neck (which definitely does not help). "The aspirin will kick in soon. But just in case, I'll brew a fresh pot of coffee for you."

I frown because I hate coffee, but when she places a mug

of the fuming black liquid in front of me, I change my mind. Just the smell of it makes me feel better.

"Thanks, Mom," I say after the first sip.

"I love you, son," she answers, drinking her coffee, too.

"You know this was the feeblest parental lecture on drinking in history, right?"

"I know."

"And that you'll probably have to resign from the Mothers' Association after this?"

"Shut up, Felipe!" she says, laughing, almost choking on her coffee.

And I smile because the hangover is starting to go away after all.

*

The whole conversation with my mom made me forget momentarily that I spent the entire night snuggling with Caio. So when he makes an appearance in the kitchen and takes a seat at the table for breakfast, it catches me off guard.

Caio has already showered and is handsome, smells great, and has a smile on his face. It's nearly insulting, considering I'm still wearing yesterday's sweaty outfit. I try to shove my nose under my armpit discreetly to gauge the situation. In case you are wondering, the situation is acceptable. Could be much worse.

"Good morning," I say, trying to pretend I wasn't just casually smelling my armpit. An armpit that, by the way, served as Caio's pillow the entire night.

Caio answers with a smile and pours himself a glass of milk. Unlike myself, he seems healthy and displays no signs of a hangover. None. Maybe he's pretending so he won't have to explain himself to my mom. Or maybe he's an expert in the hangover department, and three (or five) cans of beer have no effect on him.

I can feel the cold sweat coming down my forehead. My mom is focused on a crossword puzzle, so she's barely paying any attention to the two of us. Caio's arm bumps against mine when he reaches for the cream cheese. I look at him, he looks at me, and a never-ending look exchange takes place.

I wonder if he remembers. He probably does.

He knows he slept in my bed because he woke up still there. But does he remember the part where he hugged me and said, "Stay here with me"?

"Unforgettable," Caio says, loud and clear.

"Huh?" I say, confused, almost dropping my second cup of coffee.

"Memorable, thirteen letters," he says, pointing at my mom's crossword puzzle. "*U-N-F-O-R-G-E-T-T-A-B-L-E*," Caio spells, counting the letters on his fingers.

"Oh, thanks, dear!" my mom says, filling the blanks where Caio pointed.

I get up, frustrated, and start doing the dishes. Caio probably doesn't remember. He would probably never sleep by my side, in my bed, if he wasn't drunk. And if he does remember, I wonder if it's a story he would tell his friends when "embarrassing moments I've had with my clueless neighbor" comes up at a party.

Felipe, in ten letters: *D-E-L-U-S-I-O-N-A-L*.

*

After breakfast I decided to take a long shower. Maybe the water would make me feel better. But so far, it's brought me nothing but self-sabotage. I can't stop thinking about what Caio might be thinking, which is exhausting.

I could simply say to him, "So what did you think about last night, when we slept in the same bed for no real reason, in a super-uncomfortable position that still managed to be a pretty good experience, eh, Caio?"

But my greatest fear is to find out his answer. When you're afraid of the answer, you just don't ask the question. And that's what I do throughout the day—avoid asking the question.

Caio tries to strike up a conversation a couple of times. I give him awkward responses, looking for signs in every word he says. Most of the time, there are no signs.

I realize that I've officially ruined our friendship when Caio gives up on trying to talk to me and continues reading *The Two Towers*. This series has been an imaginary obstacle from the very beginning, and when he reads it, I go quiet, because I know he has nothing left to say.

I try to distract myself with the TV, but honestly, have you tried watching TV on a Sunday? It's torture.

So Sunday drags by. I pace around the house. Help my mom make dinner. We have ice cream for dessert. I suggest a round of Uno, but no one wants to play, and before I know it, the day is over.

I get ready for bed (shorts and an old shirt, because I decide to give my Batman pajamas a rest, but I still don't know if it's already time to wash them or not), and when I get to the bedroom, Caio is already in bed. Not my bed, unfortunately.

"You can turn off the light if you want," he says when he sees me walk in. And I feel like now is my opportunity to redeem myself. Maybe with the lights off, we'll talk for hours and clear the air, then everything will be fine again.

I turn off the lights.

Get into bed.

And then Caio turns on his phone flashlight and points it at his book, so he can keep reading. And I, obviously, want to die.

"Good night," I whisper.

I turn my back to him and will myself to sleep without waiting for an answer.

And I'm glad I don't, because there is none.

❋

I don't know how much time goes by before I feel the earthquake. I'm in the middle of a dream with Ben Affleck, which I'm not going to describe here because it's too embarrassing, and suddenly everything is shaking. I wake up with a start, and even in the pitch-black of night, I can see Caio poking my shoulder.

"Felipe! Felipe!" He's whispering, but his voice sounds desperate.

"Huh?" is all I can muster.

"I'm sorry to wake you up like this."

"It's all right," I lie, because I can't get mad at him.

"I just had to talk to someone about it, and that someone had to be you, of course. I'm too excited! There was no way I could wait until tomorrow."

"What?" I ask, feeling a streak of drool running down the corner of my mouth. I try to casually wipe it off on my collar.

"He's back!"

Your desire to snuggle with me all night? I think.

"Gandalf!" Caio explains. "He's back! I knew he was too important to die in the first book. But, you know, I was over it. And then he suddenly appears, back from the dead!"

That's when I start laughing.

Because it's so funny to see Caio genuinely excited about information that has been publicly available since 1954.

"I'm glad you're enjoying it. The book, I mean." My voice is still heavy with sleep.

"I think I'll be done reading it by the end of the week."

And then I'm attacked by the familiar feeling that the conversation is about to die. We'll be out of things to say, and I don't want to let that happen, no matter how tired I am. I find inside me the courage that I discovered yesterday (it's a little harder without the beer, but still a bit easier in the dark.)

"Do you remember?" I finally ask.

Caio doesn't seem surprised. He knows exactly what I'm talking about.

"Remember what? That I slept with you in your bed and it was kind of embarrassing? That I spent the day reading because I had no clue what to say? That I came up with this whole Gandalf-is-back thing just so I'd have an excuse to wake you up because I didn't want to go to sleep without talking to you?" he says all at once. "Yeah, I remember."

I take a relieved breath. "I was worried you might be the type who drinks and then forgets everything."

"No. I remember it all perfectly fine."

And then there's an awkward silence for almost a full minute.

"Just like that *Friends* episode where Joey and Ross sleep together on the couch without meaning to, and then they realize it was really nice. Then they start doing it in secret," I finally say.

"I've never watched *Friends*," Caio says, which is a terrible answer for so many reasons.

"But, look, relax. It's okay," I say, trying to alleviate the tension.

"I get a little needy when I drink. I'm sorry. It won't happen again."

I feel the now-familiar bucket of cold water hit me. Because I wish it *would* happen again. I wish it would happen right now, to be honest. But I don't say it. I don't say anything.

"I'm glad you're okay. I didn't want to go another day in silence. Not after I offered to be your best friend," Caio says.

And I hear his voice saying the words *best friend* inside my head two hundred times before I fall back to sleep.

DAY 11

THERE'S THE EARTHQUAKE AGAIN.

I wake up to my mom shaking me by the shoulders. It's not even eight in the morning, and I'm already in a bad mood because, seriously, what is wrong with people in this house who keep choosing to wake me up like this?

"Son, get up. I'm going to the community center today. Are you coming? I can't miss the bus," she says, not bothering to keep her voice down so my ears will comfortably receive this information.

"Huh?" I say, which is now my official answer when someone wakes me up unexpectedly.

"I'm heading to the community center. Are you coming?" my mom asks, slowly this time, like a robot.

"I'm staying home," I decide in a heartbeat.

"Okay. There's food in the fridge. Caio already had breakfast. He's coming with me. Take care, love you, bye." She kisses my forehead and doesn't give me a chance to rethink my decision.

A minute later, I hear the two of them walk out the door, and I'm alone in the house.

I already regret staying behind, but now there's nothing to be done. I turn on my side and get some more sleep.

✳

I wake up a few hours later, and the first thing I notice is the silence. This could be the part in the story when I say a bunch of nonsense about how I can *feel* the silence, or something *really* cliché like "The silence was deafening."

But what I actually realize is that I miss the quiet.

Not that Caio is a loud guest or anything. He's as quiet as I am. But Caio's presence is noisy, you know? When I'm next to him, it's as if a siren goes off inside my head. And that happens even when I'm sleeping.

In my sleep, I can still feel him in the bedroom. I try to lie in a position that won't show my belly as much, with half my brain still awake to warn me if I snore. I've been sleeping like that for the past few days, not even recognizing that I was sleeping so terribly. And now I realize how good it feels to wake up not caring if my T-shirt has rolled up and 80 percent of my body is showing. That I don't have to hide my morning wood.

I missed getting a good night's sleep.

And yet, all this soliloquy is to say that it's still weird to wake up without Caio by my side.

What kind of person am I turning into? The kind of

person who criticizes the "deafening silence" one moment, but in the next says that "Caio's presence is noisy." That's the kind of person I'm turning into.

It scares me, because this whole time I've had a crush on Caio the way one has a crush on a Hollywood celebrity. But now I can see him up close. I've heard him cry. Heard him laugh. We drank together. We *slept in the same bed together.* And I've never done that with any celebrities. Caio is real. And maybe I'm, I don't know, in love? I mean, *really* in love. Like "I want to kiss you right now but also every day" in love.

How can people be sure that they're in love, though? Is there a test?

Obviously, as I think about all that, I'm already looking up "How do I know if I'm in love?" on Google. Here are my findings:

- An article about "intrusive thoughts," which, as I've just discovered, is an obsessive passion that can make the person spend 85 percent of their life thinking about the loved one. I don't think I fit the bill. Kind of dangerous, by the way. And pretty creepy.

- A quiz from a misogynistic website claiming that if you don't mind a woman's stretch marks, then it's real love.

- A slideshow with scenes from *City of Angels* full of quotes about love.

All the results show that being in love is either sick, a serious problem, or sappy. That's not how I feel. What I feel is good.

I wish I had a best friend to talk to about it. But for the moment, I don't have any best friends who aren't actually the guy I'm in love with. In a healthy way that has nothing to do with obsessive passion, of course.

*

It's weird to think that before Caio came to stay with us, all I wanted was to spend my entire vacation locked in my room. It's now the middle of the day, and I can't stand the loneliness.

I had a frozen lasagna for lunch and started a new Netflix show about teenagers fighting to survive a zombie apocalypse. (Vampires show up in episode three.) The show is terrible, but I'm almost done with the first season.

As I'm trying to decide if I should watch another episode or take a quick nap, I hear a phone ring in my bedroom. It's not mine, that's for sure. On the nightstand, Caio's phone buzzes and blinks. I look at the screen and see Rebeca is trying to call. Caio saved her contact as "Pretty Becky <3."

I let it ring until Becky gives up, because it doesn't seem

polite to pick up someone else's phone without consent. She calls again, and once more I ignore it. But when the phone starts ringing a third time, I pick it up because A) the vibration of a phone against *any* surface annoys the heck out of me, and B) it might be an emergency.

"Hello?"

"Who's this?" she says, suspicious.

"Hey, Becky. It's Felipe. Caio went out with my mom. He forgot his phone."

"Ah, yeah," she says casually. She doesn't seem to find it weird that he's hanging out with my mom and not me. "Tell him I called, will you? If you want to add that you heard a hint of regret in my voice, that would be super helpful."

"Regret?"

"Oh, Fe. I've been a shitty friend, you know? Since I started dating Mel, I haven't been there for Caio, and when I saw you this weekend, he was so different and had so much to tell me and . . . I don't know. I felt distant. I called now to apologize. I don't want to lose him."

"No chance of that. For real, Rebeca. He adores you," I say, trying to cheer her up. "He saved your name on his phone as 'Pretty Becky' with a heart next to it.

Becky's laughter is such a pleasant sound.

"He likes you, too, Felipe. I'll admit that at first I was even jealous," she says.

"Of me? What are you talking about?"

"If only you knew. Caio told me everything about what you two have been up to. 'Felipe lent me a book here; Felipe and I watched a movie there; Felipe this, Felipe that.' I couldn't take it anymore!" she says happily.

I'm both happy and confused. Happy because Caio said nice things about me, but confused because, honestly, we haven't *done* anything since he got here. Nothing but watch TV, order takeout, and share a moment of embarrassment every time my mom says something like "I was almost a lesbian in college." I want to know everything he told Rebeca about me, but I don't know how to ask the question in a subtle way.

So I just do it directly.

"What did Caio tell you about me?" I try to make my voice sound a little ironic. But it seems like she knows exactly where I'm going with this.

"Oh, you want to know if he told me that the two of you slept in the same bed together?" she says teasingly.

So he did.

"I'm not going to play Cupid here, because I'm too old for that," Rebeca says. "But after we went to the pool on Friday, Mel told me you were smitten with Caio. I thought that was totally off because, I don't know, I don't understand you gay boys. If you were girls, you'd be married on day three and adopting a cat the following week. Are you? Smitten with him, I mean."

I go silent.

Rebeca understands my silence and keeps talking.

"And then Caio tells me you slept together but didn't do anything else, and I thought it was cute. Caio has never really liked anyone, you know? He's afraid of falling in love, his parents finding out, and all that. You've met his mom, right?"

I listen to it all attentively, imagining Caio and me adopting a cat together. I grab a piece of paper and start scribbling possible names for our cat. And Rebeca, of course, won't stop talking for one second.

"I can't tell when Caio is into someone because it has never happened before. The boy has a heart of ice. But I can guarantee he likes you. And the good news is, *I* liked you, too. Which, thank god, because I wouldn't be able to stand him talking nonstop about a guy I don't like. A point for you, Fe!"

"Thanks?" I say, trying to process all this information.

"Is that a question?"

"I don't know; I'm not good with compliments."

Rebeca ignores my comment and continues, "Here's what I mean: It's cool that you showed up. That was exactly what I meant to tell Caio if he hadn't left his phone behind.

Who forgets their phone these days? It's like leaving the house without your head! *Anyway*. I've been a pretty shitty friend, always working, studying, or making out with Melissa." Becky laughs at her own joke. "And I don't want to throw all the responsibility to you, but I'm glad that we're sharing custody of Caio now. Our high school is full of assholes; Caio hasn't made any friends since I graduated. I promise to be a better friend from now on. But take good care of him, okay? He's one of my favorite people in the whole world. Along with Melissa, my mom, and Cockroach. That's my dog, by the way. You really have to meet Cockroach one of these days. *Aaanyways*, take good care of my friend."

For heaven's sake, the girl likes to talk!

"You got it. I'll be a good friend," I promise.

"Sweet. I gotta run now. Late for work. Super late, actually. Tell Caio I called. And if you need anything, anytime, give me a ring. Actually, no, don't. Text me. I have no patience for phone calls."

"Could've fooled me," I say with a laugh.

"Jerk," she says.

We exchange phone numbers and hang up. I take a deep, relieved breath, enjoying the silence once again.

Two seconds later, I get a text from Becky (on my phone this time):

Becky:

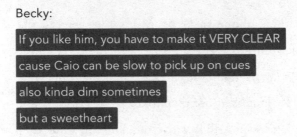

If you like him, you have to make it VERY CLEAR

cause Caio can be slow to pick up on cues

also kinda dim sometimes

but a sweetheart

I stare at my phone for a bit. Without thinking, I text thanks for the tip and send it. I reread my answer and feel it sounds a little dry. So I add a haha. And a unicorn emoji, just to be sure.

And then I prepare to spend a full day torturing myself with the possibility of Caio liking me back. And the fact that I need to make my feelings VERY CLEAR, like that, in caps.

What a disaster.

*

By the end of the afternoon, I have a list of thirty-two possible names for the hypothetical cat that Caio and I will adopt someday. My favorite at the moment are:

- Bagel, because we can call him Mini Bagel when he's being cute, and because it's one of the coolest words I know.

- Bilbo, because my story with Caio was built on *The Lord of the Rings*.

- Catsby, which would be the feline version of

Gatsby (can't stand the book; love the movie, though).

- Cheese, because I think it would be funny to have a cat named Cheese.

- Slinky, in case we adopt a fat cat. Everyone loves animals with ironic names.

Of course, creating this elaborate list didn't take my mind away from my conversation with Becky. I suddenly have all these responsibilities that I didn't have when I woke up this morning. I have a responsibility to be a good friend to Caio, to make a move if I want this story to go beyond pure friendship, and an even greater responsibility to the cats we will adopt in the future.

As anyone who has ever seen a Spider-Man movie knows, "With great power comes great responsibility" (it was actually Spider-Man's uncle who said that), but right now all I have is great responsibility and no power.

The hours drag by, and when my mom and Caio finally get home, I'm almost done watching a YouTube video where a girl throws a bunch of stuff into a giant shredder. It's mesmerizing, I swear. She throws a *fridge* into the shredder, and it turns to dust in five seconds.

"Hi, son. I missed you." My mom walks into the living room and kisses my forehead.

"Me too," Caio says, and my face goes red immediately.

I want to hurl myself into a giant shredder.

"How was it?" I ask.

My mom answers, but I'm not paying attention. I'm more focused on Caio as he rummages through his backpack, searching for something.

He produces a piece of paper and hands it to me.

"This is for you."

I unfold the paper, and a smile blooms on my face. It's another drawing by Eddie. This time, it's a self-portrait. He's wearing a Robin suit. On his costume, the *R* is inverted, and on the bottom of the page he wrote *Me*.

"Eddie missed you. He was sad when he saw you weren't with us. But I told him a new drawing would make you really happy, and he spent the whole day on that work of art," Caio says as I take in every detail of the drawing.

"It really did."

I get up and go to my room to hang the new drawing on the wall, next to the one I got last week. My bedroom is starting to look like a prekindergarten classroom, but I don't mind.

"Why did you want to stay home? If I knew, I'd have stayed, too." Caio is right behind me, and his voice is lower than usual.

"I was sleepy. No big deal. I'm sorry I aborted the mission

without saying anything," I answer, also in a low voice, as if we are sharing a secret.

"But everything's okay, right? With you, I mean. And me. We're . . . cool. Yeah?"

I have no idea what to say, so I wriggle out of it. "You left your phone behind. Becky called. Then she called two more times, and I thought it could be serious, so I picked it up."

"And was it?"

"What?"

"Serious?"

"No," I say. "And yes," I add.

"What do you mean?"

"She just wanted to say hello. But it was an important hello. She said she'll call you later."

Caio starts looking at his phone, somewhat suspicious.

"Felipe, you were on the phone for twelve minutes. No one takes twelve minutes to say hello, no matter how important it is."

"She asked me for comic book recommendations," I lie.

"Oh, yeah." Caio seems to believe my lie, and then my mom calls us to dinner.

Monday is Takeout Night, and we vote to decide what we'll eat just for the simple pleasure of turning anything about our routine into a TV game show.

I vote for Chinese because I urgently need some advice

from Grandma Thereza. But Caio and my mom prefer Mexican, and I have to accept that tonight I won't get any supernatural help from a fortune cookie.

As we eat our sophisticated Mexican dinner, sharing the tight couch and watching an episode of *Hoarders* (a really gross show to watch during a meal), Caio's phone starts ringing. He rolls his eyes and lets out an impatient sigh, but when he looks at the screen and finds out it's not his mom trying to call, his face lights up.

"It's Becky. I'll take it in the bedroom."

And off he goes, leaving half a meat burrito on a plate balancing on the couch's arm.

My mom and I continue eating in silence, completely focused on the TV. In today's episode, we're following a hoarder addicted to wedding artifacts and cats. She's never been married but has hundreds of white dresses. When the show crew finds a dead cat under a pile of bridal magazines, my mom and I exchange a look of disgust and decide it's time to watch something else.

It's been half an hour and Caio still isn't back. I can hear his voice from the bedroom but can't understand what he's saying. Sometimes he laughs out loud, but mostly it sounds like it's a serious conversation.

My mom is exhausted. She kisses me good night and goes to bed. Then it's just me, the TV, and Caio's burrito. I feel tempted to finish it, but I put it in the fridge because that seems like the right thing to do.

I go into the bedroom quietly, and Caio keeps talking to Rebeca. I try to gesture the question "Can I come in?"

"What's that?" Caio asks, taking his attention away from the phone.

Apparently, I suck at sign language.

"Can I come in?"

He smiles at me, nods, and goes back to his conversation.

"So, yeah," he says. "I'm going to hang up now. But thank you for the talk. You know exactly how to pat my head and slap me in the face at the same time."

I laugh, trying to imagine what that must feel like.

Caio hangs up and hands me a piece of paper. "I circled my favorites."

It's the list of cat names that I left on my desk.

I let out a sigh of relief, because on the top of the list I wrote only *Possible Cat Names* and not *Possible Cat Names for the Cat Caio and I Will Adopt in Our First Year of Marriage.*

I scan the list and see the names Caio circled: Nesquik, Jonas, Nugget, Beyoncé, and Bagel. The last one is the common denominator, so it's official. Our adopted cat will be named Bagel.

It's not even ten o'clock yet, but Caio is already turning off the light and getting ready for bed.

"It was exhausting today. Those kids drained all of my energy," he explains. "They won't stop for a second."

"You weren't very different," I say, remembering the afternoons I spent playing with Caio at the pool. He could run and dive for hours, never stopping to rest. But if I got tired (which happened very often), he would calm down and swim slowly with me.

Caio goes quiet for a moment and I'm starting to think he fell asleep when I hear him say in a whisper, "It was cool, wasn't it? When we were kids. At the pool and everything. Too bad it didn't last."

"It was. I don't even remember why I stopped going," I lie for the second time in the last couple of hours.

"We can go back there one of these days. I never say no to pool time. Just let me know!" he says, and I can feel a drop of sweat running down my forehead, nervous just to imagine going to the pool with Caio. "If you want to, that is," he adds, when he notices I got a little awkward.

"Tell me all the things that I missed by not being your friend for the last few years. Only the best parts," I say, trying to change the subject.

"Oh, I don't know. How old were we when we stopped hanging out every day? Twelve?"

"Thirteen."

"Whoa, thirteen years old! That was a hard time for me."

"Thirteen isn't easy for anybody," I remark.

"Sometimes you talk as if you were sixty."

"Sometimes I feel like I *am* sixty."

Caio laughs and reaches out to give my shoulder a light punch. I feel my face burn; I don't think I'll ever be ready when he touches me.

"When I was thirteen, I was in the drama club. My mom didn't know, of course. But the teacher crushed all my dreams telling me I wasn't in my element when I was acting. I got over it quickly and took dance classes. I really liked them, but then my mom found out about it and told me I had to focus on 'boy stuff.'" Caio makes air quotes on the last part.

"You're like Billy Elliot, then!" I say, excited. Because I'm crazy about Billy Elliot. And probably about Caio, too.

"Billy who?"

"The movie," I explain, a little frustrated. "About the boy who dreams of becoming a dancer, but his dad won't have it. Spoiler: At the end of the movie, his dad ends up being fine with it, Billy becomes a great dancer, and years later the movie becomes a fantastic musical with several compositions by Elton John."

"Lipé, you're a walking gay encyclopedia. I love that about you," Caio says, laughing, and I feel my hand breaking into a sweat because Caio *loves* something about me.

"I like that! Maybe I'll try to make 'walking gay

encyclopedia' into a profession!" I say. "I wonder if I can make money with it?"

"You can have your own game show on TV, testing the participants' knowledge about gay culture!" Caio suggests excitedly.

I'm smiling because it sounds like just the kind of thing my mom and I like to watch.

"Okay, practice round! Which band inspired Lady Gaga's stage name? Clock's ticking!" I almost shout.

"It was . . . It was . . ." Caio gets into character immediately. He sits on his mattress to think about it. "Queen! Queen! Queen's 'Radio Ga Ga'!" he finally yells, shaking my arm.

"Ssshhh." I try to keep it down because my mom might be asleep. "Correct. But that was an easy one, too. You have six points."

"Give me another one!" Caio says in a near whisper.

"What is Madonna's real name?"

"I need a hint," Caio says quickly.

I make up the rule on the spot. "If I give you a hint, the right answer will be worth only half the points."

"I'll take it."

"All right, then. It starts with an *M*."

"Mary . . . Jane?" he guesses.

"Incorrect! Her name is actually Madonna!"

"Not fair!" Caio whispers, trying really hard not to shout. "That was a trick question."

"Nobody said it was easy! You lose twelve points."

Caio laughs out loud. "Your points system makes absolutely no sense!"

"I know! My show, my rules. Next question," I say, taking the whole TV host character thing very seriously. "In which year was the movie *The Adventures of Priscilla, Queen of the Desert* released?"

"I need options for that one!" Caio pleads.

"All right, 1994, 1995, or 1996?"

"'94?"

"Is that your final answer?" I ask, in a terrible imitation of Regis Philbin.

"No! It's '95!"

"Wrong!" I say. "It was '94!"

"I suck at this game," Caio says, pretending to cry.

And we go on like that for quite some time. I make up questions and decide how many points each one is worth, and Caio does his best to get them all right. Sometimes I add easy questions because I'm nice and don't want to see Caio lose.

When we're done playing and my eyes finally close to sleep, I still have a smile on my face.

DAY 12

STAYING UP LATE THINKING OF gay culture trivia questions for my imaginary TV show made me wake up late today. The morning flies by, and suddenly it's already time for my weekly appointment with Olivia.

I try to organize my thoughts on the way to therapy. For the second week in a row, I have a lot to say, and it makes me anxious and a little worried.

When I get to Olivia's office (drenched in sweat, as usual), I sit in the armchair, grab a yogurt candy from the table, and don't even know where to begin.

"So, Felipe, how did the week go?" Olivia asks, kind as always.

"You'll probably think I died and was replaced by someone else," I answer. She looks puzzled. "A lot happened in the last few days. Things that never, ever, under any circumstance, have happened in my life."

Her puzzled look suddenly turns to worry, and I rush to explain.

"No, don't worry, it's nothing illegal. Well, maybe just a little bit."

"Start from the beginning, then," she says, always suggesting the most obvious option, which, up to this moment, hadn't occurred to me.

"The good news is that I completed the challenge. I talked to Caio during the day, and we talk a lot! All the time, actually. It's way easier now."

A wide smile appears on Olivia's face, and I'm happy that I'm able to elicit such an emotional response from someone like her.

"That's a good thing, Felipe. Really good," she says, pushing the jar of candy toward me so I can get another one. Apparently, that's the reward for winning the challenge. I grab another one and shove it in my pocket.

And then I start telling her about everything that happened. I talk about how good it was to hang out with Caio and meet Rebeca. Olivia seems happy that I'm making new friends. I talk about how we went to the pool together, and even though I spent the afternoon sitting in a chair just watching, I felt like part of the group, which was good. Olivia is happy that I'm widening my horizons. I even tell her about my new pajamas, but she doesn't say anything because that doesn't seem very relevant at the moment.

Finally, I get to the part I've been trying to avoid. Because

I don't know how she's going to react. But I need to put it out in the open, so I spit out one sentence after another, not even stopping to breathe.

"So. On Saturday. We went to a party. I drank beer. Jorge and Bruno showed up. I told them to go fuck themselves."

I swallow hard, waiting for the police to walk in and take me away in handcuffs for underage drinking and (maybe) because I said *fuck* in a therapy session.

"Is this the part where I should think you died and were replaced by someone else?" she says with a laugh that I wasn't expecting.

I nod.

"Tell me more about it."

And I do. The party at the square, the cans of beer, the insults, my sudden bravery . . . all of it. After listening to everything intently, Olivia takes a deep breath, scans her notes, and starts talking.

"Well, Felipe, about drinking . . ." she starts.

"I've already gotten the lecture. I've learned my lesson. I swear," I say, holding up both hands so she'll see I'm not crossing my fingers. This is probably the silliest thing I've ever done in her office.

"Okay, moving on, then. Confronting the two guys from school. Can you repeat to me exactly what you did when you felt threatened?"

"*Exactly?*" I ask.

"Yes."

"Including the curse word?"

"Felipe, trust me, I've heard much worse in this room," she says with a soft smile, and I feel more at ease.

"Okay. I stood up, looked straight at them, and said, 'Bruno, Jorge. Go fuck yourselves.' And they left." To be honest, I don't know where she's going with this.

"You got up from the table, and . . ."

"Told them to go fuck themselves?"

"No, no. Before that."

"Looked straight at them?"

And then she gives a little tap on the table, as if she's just uncovered a mystery.

"Can you see how important that is, Felipe? You looked straight at them. Not down. You faced them."

I give her a small smile because, yeah, I did. I might not remember everything in detail, but I do remember looking at them. I suddenly feel like a superhero.

"Yeah. I *did* look at them," I say, still a little astounded.

I find it amazing how therapy always makes the most obvious things seem like the discovery of the century.

"Can you tell me what motivated you to react differently this time?" Olivia asks.

"The beer?" I answer, hoping I'm wrong.

"I wonder. This might be your challenge for the week. Replay Saturday night in your head and try to figure out where that sudden bravery came from. Next week, we'll talk more about that."

I make a face. This is the first time that my challenge of the week doesn't consist of anything concrete. The challenge is basically to rethink stuff that I did and try to understand what was going through my mind at the time. I do that pretty often as it is. My entire life. I deserve a truckload of yogurt candy for that.

And then Olivia stands, and I notice that our time is up.

"No, no! Wait! I'm not done!" I say, a little too hastily.

"Felipe, unfortunately I have another patient in ten minutes. I'd be more than happy to listen to you for a bit longer, but—"

"Caio and I slept together!" I say, trying to snatch her attention. Her eyes go wide, and I go on to give her the quickest summary of the story I can muster, without forgetting the important details. "Actually, we didn't *sleep*-sleep together. We just slept in my bed. The two of us, together, in the same bed. And we fell asleep like that. And the next day—oh, god—it was a never-ending embarrassment, because I had no idea what that meant. Then we talked and apparently it didn't mean anything. But then I freaked out and realized that I might be in love. And it's not like what we feel for hot guys in movies. This is real, and it might amount to something in the end. And then Becky called, and she thinks I have to make it clear that I'm into him. And I have no idea how to do that. Because I'm afraid he'll say no. Because I'm afraid of a lot of stuff, actually. Because, you know . . . I'm fat." When I'm done saying all of this, my voice sounds weak.

Olivia takes a couple of notes on her notepad, then checks the clock, and her phone starts ringing. It's the receptionist. The next patient is already here.

"Felipe. We've talked about this during so many sessions, and I am very proud to see how much you are growing. It's normal to be afraid. It's normal to want people's approval," she says as she walks me to the door. "And being in love is great. Don't think of it as a curse. Use this opportunity to get to know yourself better. Think about this week's challenge."

"Any last-minute advice?" I ask, desperate, half my body already out of the room.

"There's no need for fear," she says with a smile.

And I walk out with the feeling that I've heard that before.

*

I'm in the town library. Olivia's final bit of advice brought me here.

I don't really know how to explain the way my brain works, but when I walked out of the office, I immediately started walking toward the library. It was here that my grandmother Thereza worked her whole life. It was here that I spent most of my childhood, when my grandma used to pick me up from school and bring me along with her because my mom was too busy at work.

I know every corner of this library, and as soon as I push open the heavy glass door, I can smell the books. The smell brings a lot of memories, and I smile because most of them are good.

"Felipe?" I hear a voice call out, and find a lady sitting behind the counter at the reception desk. It's Marta. She's always worked here at the library. She and my grandma were really close. When Marta greets me with a warm smile on her face, I realize how much I've missed her and didn't even know it.

"Hi, Marta! How great to see you here," I say, leaning against the counter.

"Oh, my boy. I'm always here. My children want to push me into retirement, but I can't leave the books behind. What about you? How are you doing? You never come to visit anymore." She says it jokingly, but I feel a sting of guilt.

I realize that I haven't been back since my grandma died.

"It's true. I've just been so busy. With school and everything. But now I'm on vacation. I came to catch up and to look for an important book. One that I'm sure I'll find here."

Marta starts rolling up her sleeves right away, ready to help me with my search.

"All right, which book do you need? Is it for school? It must be for history, no? Boys your age will only show up if they're looking for some historical thing. It seems as if they haven't been able to put all of history online yet."

"No, no. It's not for school. I think I can find it myself. That is, if everything is still in the same place."

"Everything here is still the same; nothing has changed." Then she takes one look at me, and I think she remembers that my grandma isn't here anymore. "Well, almost nothing."

Marta pats my shoulder, and that's my cue to start my search. I walk down the main hall (so empty it's almost scary) and stop at the end, to the left, at the children's books section.

I run my fingers down the book spines on the top shelf, searching one by one. It doesn't take me long to find the old, yellowed edition of *The Wonderful Wizard of Oz*, and when I take it off the shelf, I feel the memories coming back little by little.

I was ten or eleven that day. Right when being fat started becoming a reason for the boys in my class to make fun of me. My grandma came to pick me up early from school. I don't remember if it was Indigenous Peoples' Day or Easter, but I remember I wasn't wearing my normal clothes. So, accordingly, it was either an offensive headpiece made of paper or not-so-offensive bunny ears. You can pick your favorite to imagine the story from here on.

Anyway, we were walking down the square on our way to the library when we saw a group of kids from school on the playground. I remember it had just been renovated and there was a line of kids waiting to use the new metal slide that would burn our butts on hot, sunny days.

"Want to go play with the boys for a bit?" Grandma asked, pointing at a group of boys from my class. Boys who, at the time, already had a list of nicknames for me and would use that list all the time, without thinking twice. Because when you're ten or eleven, you don't care.

"No. Let's go to the library," I answered, pulling my grandma in the opposite direction.

"Do you want to go play with the *girls*, then?" she asked, and at the time I didn't understand what she meant. Now I do.

"I don't want to go, Grandma. Let's get out of here," I whimpered like a brat to see if that would work. She took my hand, and we kept on walking.

"You need to make more friends, Lipé. I was just trying to help. Grandma's sorry," she said.

"I don't think I want to be friends with them."

"May I know why?"

"I don't know, Grandma. I don't feel well. That's all."

"What is it that you do feel?" Grandma asked, and I think that was my very first therapy session.

"Afraid," I answered without thinking. And my grandma went silent, not knowing what to say. I also wouldn't know what to tell a ten- or eleven-year-old who's *afraid* of his classmates. Maybe I'd call the police.

All I remember is, on that day, when we got to the library, my grandma handed me this edition of *The Wonderful Wizard of Oz* (which at the time was already old).

"There's a scared lion in this book. He learns to be brave. Maybe you can, too," Grandma Thereza said, stroking my head as I scanned the illustrations on the pages, searching for a quick answer that wouldn't involve me reading the entire book.

Grandma was always like that. She always had the right book for the right occasion. And I, with nothing else to do that afternoon, sat in an armchair and started reading. I remember reading until my head hurt, and at the end of her workday, I hadn't finished yet. I took the book home, where I read it to the end.

At the end, the Lion kills a giant spider that was scaring all the animals. He's then crowned as the new king of the forest.

Right after he kills the spider, he says proudly, "You need fear your enemy no longer."

That part was stuck in my head forever. I read and reread it, trying to put myself in the Lion's shoes. Trying to see a way to defeat my giant spider and be crowned the king of school. For days I went to school determined to face the spiders, but when the time came, I always put my head down and listened in silence as my schoolmates chanted, "Chubby, fat, punching bag."

Six or seven years later, the solution hasn't come to me yet. And today in therapy, when I heard Olivia say those words, I thought I could find the answer here.

"I'm borrowing this one," I tell Marta, sliding the book across the counter.

"*The Wonderful Wizard of Oz*? One of my favorites. We have a newer edition. Revised, all illustrated, exquisite. Would you like me to get it?"

"No, no need, Marta. I'm taking this one right here. It's special."

Marta thinks for a second and then comes closer to me, as if about to tell me a secret. As if the library wasn't almost completely empty.

"If it's that special, you can keep it. But don't tell anyone I let you do that."

Even though it's an old, yellow book with some loose

pages, it's one of the best gifts I've ever received. So I don't bother being coy and accept it right away.

"Thank you so much, Marta. I swear I'll come to visit more. Even if I don't have to return this one," I say, waving the book in the air.

"Yes, do come back. If you come at three o'clock, I can even offer you a cup of coffee," she says sweetly.

We say our goodbyes and I take off.

✳

It's weird to come home from therapy and find Caio there. Even though he's been staying here for over ten days, I'll never get used to opening the door and finding him here, waiting for me.

Well, technically not *waiting* for me, but let me dream.

When I see him, he's lying on the couch reading, and judging by the silence, I already know my mom isn't home.

"I'm so glad you're home! I couldn't take it anymore!" Caio says as soon as he sees me walk in the door. "Your mom left and spent the whole afternoon out, and I've been alone this entire time. I thought I'd die of boredom, if that's even possible."

It's possible.

And I know this because I've looked up "Can you die of boredom?" and discovered that yes, yes you can. My online search history is embarrassing, and I know it.

"How was therapy?" Caio asks, dragging me back from my thoughts.

"Ah, it was good. Olivia was proud of how things went this week."

"Such as . . . ?"

"Such as telling Jorge and Bruno to go fuck themselves," I answer without skipping a beat.

Caio seems shocked. "She was *proud*? I need to meet this Olivia!"

"Oh, and there was also the weekly challenge, which I won! The one where I had to talk to you, you know."

"And? Did you get a reward?" Caio asks excitedly.

"I did, but it wasn't a big deal. Still, I saved one for you." I take the yogurt candy from my pocket and throw it to him.

Caio catches it, still excited, and makes space for me on the couch.

"I can't keep the whole thing," he says.

"But you helped me. And I promised you'd get a prize."

"Your challenge was to talk to me during the day, right?" he asks, and I feel ridiculous because who needs a therapist to be able to act like a normal human being and have a conversation?

Apparently, me.

"Yeah, that's what it was," I answer.

"So my job was merely to exist. And to listen. You did most

of the work!" Caio says, opening the wrapper and biting half the candy.

"I think your share of it was to trust me and not think I'd lost my mind," I say.

"You haven't lost your mind. Not because of that, anyway."

"So there are *other* reasons?" I laugh.

"Exactly. And one of them is that you've elected not to share this delicious prize with me," Caio says, holding out the other half of the candy and wiggling his eyebrows in a way that's simultaneously funny and, I don't know, enticing.

"Okay, I'll take my share," I say, rolling my eyes and holding out my hand to grab my half.

And then the weirdest thing happens.

Because Caio doesn't hand me the candy.

He goes to put it directly into my mouth.

And, reflexively, I just open it.

And for a second, the tips of his fingers are *inside* my mouth.

And this is the weirdest, most wonderful experience I've had in the last few years.

But, of course, my mom arrives at that exact moment, and the noise of her key turning the lock makes me jump, sending the candy straight to the back of my throat. I start coughing and can barely breathe. When the door opens, my mom finds Caio pulling my arm up and slapping my back, my face going red as I try to spit out the piece of candy.

Despite the choking that almost got me killed (I'm fine now, thanks for asking), I think my mom's arrival was timely. Because I wouldn't know how to deal with the immediate consequences of Caio placing a piece of candy inside my mouth.

What do people usually do in this kind of situation? Do they lick the other person's finger? Give it a little nibble, maybe? I'd probably have had a nervous breakdown, so, yeah. Thanks, Mom.

*

Right after she came home, my mom made dinner. We ate in front of the TV by force of habit, and now, lying in bed and ready to sleep, the candy episode seems like a distant memory.

And I choose to believe that.

"So what's the challenge this week? Anything I can help with?" Caio says, turning off the lights and settling on the mattress by my bed.

"I think this time I'll have to figure it out myself," I say.

"Why?"

"The challenge isn't exactly something I have to *do*. It's more like something I need to *think about*. To find out, actually. I need to find the trigger that gives me the courage to,

I don't know, do things I normally wouldn't. Something I need to find inside myself. It's a little confusing."

"Whoa." Caio seems surprised.

"Yeah. I won't be able to figure it out in one week. I think it'll be longer than that."

"Like a month?" Caio asks optimistically.

"Like a lifetime," I answer realistically.

"And do you know where to begin this search?"

"I think I do. I'm not sure. I got a book from the library today that might help me out. My grandma told me to read it when I was a kid, and at the time, I don't think I really got what it was about."

"Which one?"

"*The Wonderful Wizard of Oz.* Have you read it?"

"Yeah. I mean. Actually, no. I know the story, though. *The Wonderful Wizard of Oz* is like the book everyone says they've read even though they haven't."

"Caio, I can't believe you're that kind of person," I say in a funny voice to pretend I'm shocked. (I actually am, a little bit.)

"Are you going to tell me you've never done that?"

"Never! It's one of the worst character flaws."

"Character flaw?" Caio is the one feigning shock now.

"Relax, everyone has one or two," I answer, trying to calm him down.

"What are yours?"

"Sometimes I walk into the elevator and press the button really quick so the door will close, even though I know there are other people coming, because I hate to share elevator space," I admit.

"Monster," Caio answers.

"Your turn," I say, turning this conversation into the Character Flaw Game.

"Okay. Sometimes I don't wash my glass after drinking water, because water can't make things dirty," he says.

"Who'd throw the first stone for that one?" I ask. "Sometimes I accept flyers on the street and then throw them out in the first garbage can I can find."

"Sometimes I look at the phone screen of the person sitting next to me on the bus and judge them if the wallpaper is a photo of themself."

"Yes!" I yell. "I can't fathom the amount of self-confidence required to need to see one's own face when looking at the time."

"Sometimes, when my mom isn't looking, I drink juice straight from the container." Caio keeps admitting things as if this is the most fun game on the planet.

"Sometimes I put bubble gum under my desk at school."

"Sometimes I flip over the doormat outside apartment 55 because I hate the woman who lives there."

"Mrs. Clélia?" I ask.

"The one and only."

"I hate her, too."

And we confess the night away. At no point do I find the courage to confess to more, um, *serious* stuff. But it's fun to tell him things that no one else knows about me.

When the confessions get too gross ("Sometimes I take a booger from my nose and play around with it in my fingers before throwing it out, because there are times when the texture feels really good" were Caio's precise words), I feel like it's time to stop.

"Okay, no more confessions for the time being, because I want to continue to believe you are a good person," I tell him.

"Yeah, I better stop right here," Caio answers. "I don't want you to wake up tomorrow hating me forever."

As if that were possible.

DAY 13

FOR SOME REASON, I can't sleep well. Around three in the morning, I wake up from a restless sleep, and in an attempt to relax, I pick up *The Wonderful Wizard of Oz* from my nightstand. I start reading it under my phone's flashlight.

Well, then it's nearly six a.m., I've finished the book, and the story wasn't much help in my journey to find my inner courage. If anything, reading the book after all this time annoyed me. I didn't remember the magician being such an asshole.

The courage that the Cowardly Lion was looking for was always inside him, that's for certain. But instead of saying, "Dude, your courage is inside you," the Wizard gives him a green liquid to drink, as if it were a potion. The Lion drinks it, feels brave, and becomes king of the forest. And he'll probably never know that the green liquid had absolutely *nothing* in it. So, the Wizard is an asshole.

Caio is asleep on his mattress, curled up under a blanket and snoring softly. I wonder how many gallons of courage potion I'd need to hold his hand. To say, "I like you, and I want to kiss you." To *actually* kiss him, if he allowed me to.

My head feels like it's about to explode at any moment, so I do what any sensible person would in my situation: run to my mom.

I leave my room quietly, so as not to wake up Caio, then slowly creep into hers. I even give her door a light knock, but I don't wait for an answer.

The room is still dark, despite the slightly open window. I step slowly toward her queen bed, which is only half-occupied, treading carefully so as not to trip on any shoes that might be lying on the floor.

"Mom?" I say in a quiet voice, lying by her side and pulling the floral comforter over my body.

"Is everything all right, Felipe?" She's still half-asleep, but her hand moves straight to my forehead to check my temperature. It must be some mom emergency protocol, I don't know.

"Yeah, everything's fine. I just wanted to stay here for a bit."

"It's been a while since you stayed here with me. You were still little the last time," she says, pulling me in for a hug.

When she does that, I feel small again. Not in a bad way. I feel protected. It's as if I could say anything and still be sure it would be okay. And then, without second-guessing myself, I blurt out, "I think I'm in love."

"With Caio?" my mom says without hesitation.

"Is it that obvious?"

"Speaking as someone who brought you into this world and who lives in this house, yes. Pretty obvious," she says, smiling.

"That's what I was afraid of."

"Afraid of?" She seems confused.

"If it's that obvious to you, it must be obvious to him, too, Mom! And if he hasn't made a move yet, then that's definitely because—"

"Because he's shy. Or afraid that his mother will find out. Or maybe he's intimidated because you're the handsomest guy in the world," she interrupts.

"You're my mom. It's your job to say I'm the handsomest guy in the world," I say, rolling my eyes.

"Son, look at me," she says, turning in bed to face me. "You may think I'm saying this because I'm your mother. And you're partially right, of course. I will always think you are the handsomest boy in the world, because I'm your mother. But beauty is not only here," she says, running her hand down my face.

I don't know if it's the nice, warm bed, or if it's my mom's tender touch, but a tear escapes from my eye. A happy one, for a change.

"I'm so proud of who you are. Of the decisions you make,

of how you face your challenges, of how you make me laugh even when my day sucks. You are my companion, son. And anyone who can enjoy your company is lucky. And I'm very happy that you trust me enough to tell me about your feelings," she says, wiping my tear with the tip of her finger.

"Thanks, Mom. But I only came to you because I have no other friends," I tease.

"Unbelievable! Get out of here." She laughs and pushes me away.

Then we're laughing and pushing each other, and it feels so good. I wish I knew how old is too old to lie down in your mom's bed and talk. I hope there's no such thing, because I want to be able to do this always.

"So, then, what do I have to do to . . . you know . . . *get* him?" I ask, a little embarrassed that I'm asking *my mom* for romantic advice.

"Why would *I* know, Felipe? If I were good at flirting, you wouldn't be here right now, because this half of the bed would be taken," my mom answers, raising her eyebrows.

"Mom!" I yell, embarrassed, because it's so weird to imagine a dude lying here in her bed.

"It's true, son. I gave up on dating long ago. Doesn't mean I don't get around every once in a while. I'm not dead, you know?"

"Mooom! You're not helping!" I say, louder, because it's

even weirder to imagine that another dude has probably been here.

"Okay, I don't know how to help. I haven't had a lot of romances that have worked out, obviously, but I can help with the ones that didn't. So you can learn from my mistakes. How noble of me!" She leans on her elbows and looks at me.

"Right, share your wisdom, Mom." I adopt a meditation pose that makes no sense, but I think it is funny because my mom muffles a laugh.

"Okay, tip number one: Don't fall for guys who are ashamed of telling their friends about you. They're either assholes or married."

Apparently, Caio has been telling Becky all about me, so one point for Caio.

"Number two." My mom raises two fingers. "The guy might be the hunkiest in the whole world, but if you can't talk to him for more than half an hour without wondering if you can die of boredom, that beauty isn't worth much."

Yes, Caio is handsome, but I'm never bored when I talk to him. Good sign, right? Best of both worlds. Another point for Caio!

"And finally, number three. This one is really important, so pay attention. Don't fall in love with someone who doesn't make *you* feel beautiful. I don't mean it has to be someone who always tells you that you're perfect and wonderful. Not at all. But when you feel good-looking just by being close to them, then, my son, it's much easier. You wake up with bed-head, your face all crumpled, and yet you still feel handsome. Because you're with someone who isn't pointing out your flaws. Who doesn't make you feel worse. Doesn't point out that stretch mark on your butt that you hadn't even noticed until that moment. Because the person who sees past the sur-face sees the best in you," she says, proud of her wisdom.

I think of how I feel when I'm with Caio. Definitely not handsome. But pleasant, funny, and a little anxious. Anxious in a kind-of-good, kind-of-bad way. But *handsome* hand-some . . . I can't say I've felt that way yet.

"Is this advice based on fact?" I pry.

"Of course! Each relationship that goes wrong always teaches us a lesson. So far, I've learned three. Ricardo, Luiz Antonio, and your father. In that order."

I'm shocked. "Luiz Antonio . . . my gym teacher?"

"Shut up, and let's go have some breakfast," she says, jumping out of bed.

✻

I'm washing the dishes after lunch, Caio is drying them, and my mom is on a chair filing her nails like a baroness.

"It's Wednesday! What'll be our movie for Musical Wednesdays?" Caio asks, genuinely excited as he puts away a plate in the cabinet.

"Caio, please, don't let my mom believe that these themed weeknights are cool," I say. "You're creating a monster, and after you leave, I'll be the one left behind to deal with her!"

"Don't mind him, Caio," my mom says, standing up and putting her nail file away. "Even after your parents are back from their trip, you can always come here every Wednesday to honor our commitment to musicals. If you want to, of course!"

That leaves me trying to come up with themes for the whole week, just so I can get Caio to come over every day.

"Of course I do. I can't live without Musical Wednesdays anymore!" he says.

"But today I'm going to disappoint the two of you," my mom says with a pout. "Too much work, tight deadline. I can't watch a movie. But you know what? I've just had an idea."

"Mom, please don't try to make Catwalk Fridays happen again," I say.

Caio laughs out loud.

"That wouldn't be a bad idea. But today I want the two of you to have fun. Have Musical Wednesday without me. Far from here. At the movies, just the two of you. All on me," she says, getting money from her bra (not kidding) and putting some bills in my back pocket.

"Whoa, thanks, Rita!" Caio says excitedly.

"Thanks, Mom," I say, shaking with anxiety.

"No need to thank me, boys," she says with a wink directed at me. Not at all in a discreet way, which makes me even more nervous.

✳

"Well, I'm okay with *Zombie Robots: The Attack 2*," Caio says, looking up at the billboard with all the showtimes.

We could have predicted that this Musical Wednesday would turn out not to be all that musical. Our town's movie theaters don't show any musicals. I don't think the locals are quite the right audience for that. Or for subtitles, apparently. *Zombie Robots: The Attack 2* is the only subtitled movie available today, and the other options aren't exactly exciting:

- *Screwball Mother-in-Law* is a Brazilian comedy with a decidedly unfunny cast.

- *Passion of Fire and Light* is a film adaptation of a bestselling novel about a psychic teenager who falls in love with a ghost who then tries to be reincarnated in someone else's body so they can be together forever, but he ends up being reincarnated as fire. Really. He becomes *fire itself.* And the girl is still in love with him. In love with the element of fire.

- *Forest Gone Wild!* is a low-budget animated film with talking animals.

See what I mean?

"I've never watched *Zombie Robots: The Attack 1*, but fine by me." My hands are sweaty. Because, in theory, this is a date. Our first date. It might all go wrong, but for some reason I believe this night might be—

"The beginning," Caio says.

"What?"

"The first movie is called *Zombie Robots: The Beginning.*"

"Hollywood makes no sense," I decide, and get in line for the tickets.

"Can we get popcorn?" Caio asks when I come back with our two tickets.

"Yeah! Which one do you want?"

"Maybe a large with butter to share? Oh, no! Never mind. You don't like it with butter. So get a medium just for me."

I'm surprised because I don't even remember telling him that I don't like butter on my popcorn.

We stand in the line for popcorn, which is longer than we could have anticipated for a Wednesday afternoon. Kids are running and screaming all around us, acting out a kid's version of *The Hunger Games*. Impatient parents roll their eyes at other people's kids and try to keep their own kids by their sides. It's probably the combination of school break and *Forest Gone Wild!*

When it's finally my turn, I order the two popcorns, and

even though they're both medium, I get "the look" from the cashier. When you're fat, there are two variations of "the look" that you might get in food-related situations:

1. The look you get when you order a small means, "You're that big and you're trying to watch what you eat?"

2. The look you get when you order a large means, "You're that big and you *still* can't stop eating?"

All of which is to say that if you're fat, you're never right.

I try not to mind the look for now. In the end, it's not too hard because Caio is so excited to spend the next couple of hours watching robot zombies on a giant screen that I end up feeling excited, too.

When we enter, the movie theater is almost empty. There are some couples scattered around the sides, an elderly man who came to the movies by himself, and a group of friends, laughing hysterically. We go straight to the back of the the-ater (because I'm tall and don't want to be in anyone's way), and when I sit down, I curse the designer of this movie the-ater's chairs under my breath. Or of movie theaters in gen-eral. The person who came up with this seat definitely did not consider the existence of people my size.

I take a seat, uncomfortably, my legs squeezed by the row

in front and my arms without room to move freely. I look like a T. rex holding a popcorn bucket. Caio is sitting to my right, and he seems relaxed and comfortable. I think about complaining about the size of these seats with Caio, just to vent, but when I open my mouth, the lights go off and the trailers begin.

My hands automatically break into a sweat, and I eat some popcorn to put my mind at ease. The movie starts, and after half an hour I realize that I haven't been paying attention to anything. My leg is shaking, and I try to coordinate its rhythm with the explosions on the screen.

The group of friends in the theater talks loudly during the movie, but no one seems to mind. Some couples are kissing in a very, um, intimate way. And the older man who was by himself already left, probably offended by the low quality of the special effects in *Zombie Robots: The Attack 2.*

An hour later, I realize I'm done with my popcorn, and I haven't had one sip of my soda. My mouth is dry, and I reach out to grab the Coke resting in the cup holder by my side. The Coke is watery, the ice is all melted, but it's still refreshing.

When I finally let go of the cup and am about to go back to my original T. rex pose, placing my hands on my belly to try and take up less space, it happens.

Caio leans against my arm, slides his fingers down to my

hand, and squeezes it. I hold back an anxious breath, not quite sure what's going on. We're holding hands, and from that moment on, I officially cannot pay any attention to the robot zombies destroying the human race. Because Caio and I are holding hands. Because my hand is gross with sweat. And yet, he won't let go.

I want to glance to the side and see what face Caio is making as he holds my hand. But I can't bring myself to do it. I stare instead at the movie screen and watch the images flash by one after the other, but I don't care about any of them.

Time flies, and I get the sense that the movie is about to end. The hero saved the planet from the zombies and finally rescued his girlfriend. The two of them meet in a postwar scene. He's all dirty and manly; she's all proper, wearing makeup and short-shorts despite the apocalypse. They kiss, and that's when Caio squeezes my hand a little harder. It's not quite a crunch. More like a light pressure. But I believe it's a sign. A sign that I'm the sweaty hero he'd like to kiss. Or a sign that the movie is about to end, and he'd like to let go of my hand.

I open my fingers slightly, giving him the freedom to let go. But he doesn't. That's a good thing.

The movie ends, the credits start rolling. But the lights don't come back on because apparently it's illegal to create

225

movies without scenes after the credits now. So no one budges. The whole audience just sits there, listening through a bad Linkin Park song that's probably featured on the soundtrack of *Zombie Robots: The Attack 2*. My heart is beating with the rhythm of the fast and heavy music, but when Caio slides his finger down the back of my hand, my heart skips a beat.

It's hard to focus on anything other than the touch of his hand. I feel like time is passing and I need to make a move, quickly. I look up at the credits, and what I see is:

Make it clear that you like him.
—Becky

Be Brave.
—Grandma

Caio is a little slow, but he's a sweetheart.
—Becky, again

There's no need to be afraid anymore.
—the Cowardly Lion (and also my therapist)

Your capabilities are as big as your courage.
—any self-help book

So I take a deep breath. Squeeze Caio's hand really tight, not caring if I'm hurting him or not. (I probably am.) And look at him.

When I turn my face, I find he's already looking at me. I don't know for how long, but there he is. Waiting for me. The refrain of the song from the movie credits is already in its third cycle. I don't have a lot of time.

I bite my lip.

Close my eyes.

And kiss Caio.

He kisses me back, and I try to manage the right amount of tongue and saliva. It's not the perfect kiss, like the ones I always see in movies, because A) it tastes like butter, and B) Linkin Park is playing. But I never thought kissing would be like this. It's a nice, slippery feeling. Caio's lips are soft but not flabby. They're like gummy bears. And from the way he's kissing me, it seems I'm not too bad, either.

I don't know how long our kiss lasts, but when we separate, we both look at the movie screen. The post-credits scene is almost done. We still have a little while.

So we kiss each other again.

We're a kissing machine.

Kissing zombie robots.

I don't ever want to stop, but when the lights come on, we do.

The theater is empty except for the cleaning guy who's sweeping the first row and pretending we're not there.

We get up at the same time. I drop my empty popcorn bucket. I try to crouch to pick it up, but the space is too tight. I decide to let it go and leave, and then I trip over my own bucket and drop my empty soda cup, too. I'm such a disaster.

When we leave the movies, I feel my face burning. I want to scream, but I don't know if that would be appropriate. I also don't know if it's humanly possible to sweat the way I'm sweating right now.

Caio lets out a loud sigh, and I look at him. His hair is a mess (which might be a little bit my fault), but he's more gorgeous than ever. His face opens into a perfect smile, and I'm surprised because I never thought a normal person would react that way after kissing me. I've always imagined tears of regret. Or fainting. Or throwing up.

"Wow," I say.

"Wooow," he says, stretching the word.

"Wanna come over to my place?" I say, because I'm feeling comical.

"Do I have a choice?" Caio gives my shoulder another one of his weird punches.

So we walk home. It's already dark by the time we leave the mall, and the sky is full of stars. I look up and thank Becky for the push, Olivia for the advice, L. Frank Baum for writing *The Wonderful Wizard of Oz*, my grandma for having existed, and the people who invented scenes after movie credits and armrest supports that can be moved.

Without all of you, none of this would have been possible.

*

This might not be news for anyone, but I'm not good at dealing with things.

All I know about first kisses I learned from books, movies, and TV shows. A first kiss matters because, in comedies, it's the moment we've all been waiting for. In movies where the world is ending, it's that "I can't die before I kiss you!" moment. In reality TV shows, it's just a test to see if two people are a good match.

But in my life, my first kiss happened with the most gorgeous guy who has ever set foot on this planet and who, conveniently, is staying over at my place. In my bedroom. By my side. So what happens now?

It wasn't meant to be this way. Not for us to kiss and then go to sleep in the same room just a few hours later. This doesn't happen when you're seventeen and live with your mother. Maybe I'm just lucky.

But lucky or not, I can't keep calm.

It all runs through my head as we walk home. I try to start a conversation about the movie, but then I realize that I don't remember anything that happened in it. Caio doesn't seem to remember, either. The tension between us as we walk is good but still tense enough to be called *tension*.

There's no way not to notice the elephant in the room.

When we get home, my mom is waiting on us for dinner.

"Finally! I'm starving, but I didn't want to eat by myself. I think I'm needy today," she says as soon as we open the door, with a little wink my way. I want to die.

Even though I ate all that popcorn, I don't say no to my mom's dinner. She asks how the movie was, and I shove a forkful of rice and beans in my mouth, because I don't know how to answer.

"You know, right? Zombies who turn into robots. Can't expect too much from it," Caio answers, and smiles at me.

My mom seems satisfied with the answer.

We're doing our usual routine of dinner and TV, and my mom doesn't seem happy with anything that's on. She keeps pressing the remote compulsively, zapping through all the channels, and I swear that between one show and another, I am able to spot about five couples kissing.

My embarrassment gets worse and worse.

I glance over at Caio, and he seems anxious. His legs shake to the speed of the changing channels on the TV, and I'm startled when he gets up suddenly from the couch.

"I'm done. I'm tired. I think I'm gonna go to bed," he

announces hurriedly, and disappears before I can get a word in edgewise.

My mom and I sit there in silence. On the TV there's an ad about a new collection of hits by Alcione Nazareth, a famous samba singer.

"Tell me everything!" she says in a low voice, elbowing my side as if we were best friends from school.

"We kissed," I say in an even lower voice, and my mom holds back a scream.

This is one of the weirdest moments of my life. Because I just said I kissed Caio (and that is a TRUE STATEMENT!). Because I'm talking about it *with my mom*! And, more important, because Alcione's music is on TV.

"So, what's it going to be? Are you two together? Can I call him my son-in-law?" she says excitedly, like a child who just won a trip to Disney.

"Sssssshhhhh. No need to scream!" I say, because Caio can definitely hear all of this from the bedroom. "Now I have no idea what to do. I'm not an expert in . . . *kissing*."

My mom goes serious all of a sudden, looking deeply into my eyes. She grabs my two hands and strokes me with the tips of her fingers.

"Son, no matter what happens, I want you to know that there are condoms in the second drawer of my nightstand."

"Mom!" I shout, letting go of her hands.

I get up from the couch and almost run to my room, because I'd rather deal with a recently kissed Caio than with this conversation.

*

Caio is in bed scrolling on his phone, but as soon as I walk into the room, he drops it and stares at me.

No pressure.

"What a day, huh?" he says as I turn off the lights and lie in bed.

"Today I discovered my mom once dated my gym teacher," I say, because despite everything that happened, it's another piece of information that I still haven't been able to fully process.

"Was that before or after we kissed, and I acted like a fool because no one has ever kissed me and then taken me home on the very same day?"

"That was before," I answer, laughing.

"Just to be clear, no one has ever taken me home in general, okay? Under no circumstances. If you know what I mean," Caio says, a little embarrassed by his confession that he's a virgin.

Ha. Ha.

I decide to be honest, too. "What about me? Who, until today, had never kissed anyone?"

"No one?" Caio asks, seemingly scared, as if I am

good-looking enough to have a line of people trying to kiss me at all times.

"You were my first," I say, and my forehead starts sweating when I confess the truth. Caio was my first kiss. It's still too surreal for me. I'm afraid I'll suddenly wake up to find out I've been sent to a parallel dimension by mistake, and that I need to return to my universe where I suck and no one wants to kiss me.

I don't want to go back.

"I hope I didn't disappoint you," Caio says.

"I hope I didn't, either."

I don't know at what point this happened, but I let my hand fall off the side of my bed, and Caio interlaced his fingers with mine. We're in the dark, holding hands, staring at the ceiling, and saying anything that pops into our heads.

"Counting you, I've kissed two mouths in my life," Caio informs me. "So far, you're way ahead. The other one was the biter."

"Denis." I nearly whisper the name of the first guy Caio kissed. Which, if you stop to think about it, is a pretty creepy thing to do this late at night.

"You remember his name?" Caio laughs.

"I'm good with remembering names," I answer, even though that's not true. I think I just have a good memory for resentment.

"No need to be jealous of Denis. I haven't talked to him since then. And like I said, you were better," Caio says, trying to steer the conversation in a different direction.

"I'm not a jealous guy," I say, but deep down, I think I am.

What has this kiss done to me that I can't stop lying for one second?

"It's a funny thing," he says. "We just kissed today, and we're already talking about jealousy. That's not right. There must be something else between the first kiss and the first bout of jealousy."

"Probably a little more kissing," I joke, but Caio doesn't need any more to jump into my bed.

In the dark bedroom, he catches me by surprise and squeezes himself between me and the edge of the bed. The first three seconds are a hot mess because he tries to kiss my mouth but first hits my nose and chin.

When our lips finally meet, I'm certain I want to do this every day. But then Caio hugs me, and his hand touches my hips, and I know it's time to stop.

I have to say, kissing in the movies is very different from kissing in bed, in total darkness. Here in my bedroom, Caio kisses me intently. I try to kiss him back in the same way, but my mind is on full alert because there are parts of my body he's not allowed to touch. That *no one* is allowed to touch.

His hands slide up and down my hips. I furtively try to keep my T-shirt in place. I pull it down on one side, he pulls it up from the other, and all of a sudden, kissing Caio is almost exhausting.

When our lips separate, I'm breathless. I need more training to synchronize kissing and breathing. Caio runs his hand down my face, which sends shivers down my neck, and before he can say anything, I say, "I'm not ready yet."

Caio looks confused. "Ready for what?"

"Oh, for god's sake, Caio! Don't make me say it."

"To be in a relationship?" he asks.

"No! To have sex!" I say, almost whispering the last word.

"Are you afraid your mom is going to walk in on us?"

"No, my mom isn't the problem," I say. "She'd probably throw a pack of condoms our way and bring some juice after we were . . . done."

Caio laughs and runs his fingers through my hair, and I discover that, after the kiss, this is the best thing I've felt today.

"I'm sorry. I didn't want to go all the way today. I was just excited and got ahead of myself. I don't want to make you uncomfortable. I'm sorry. For real." He says all of that propped on my left arm, looking me in the eye.

I'm living through one of the most surreal moments of my life, and I feel like diving completely into it. But usually diving completely into it means letting the other person touch you, and I don't know if I'm ready for that.

"It's okay. I just need a little more time," I say, running my hand through his hair, too, the way I've already done a couple hundred times before in my imagination. "In the meantime, we can do a lot of other stuff together."

"Like what?"

"Like go on a date, I don't know. Talk about everything, get to know each other better," I say, trying to use everything I've learned from all the rom-coms I've watched in my life.

"Felipe, technically, I've been going on a date with you for thirteen days now."

"And there are two more to go," I say, with a smile that I'm not sure he can see in the darkness of the room.

"Actually, just one more. My parents come back on Friday morning," he says.

I know it doesn't make a difference which day he's leaving because we live in the same apartment building, but I can't help but feel sad. Because it won't be the same when he goes back to apartment 57. I'll miss his company. I'll miss sleeping like this, really close to him. I'll miss grabbing his hand and placing it on my face, because I don't want him touching any-thing from my neck down (which, by the way, is exactly what I'm doing right now).

"I'm sorry if I made things weird," I say.

"I'm sorry if I pushed your boundaries," he says.

"I'm sorry I'm such a weirdo."

"I'm sorry if I made you feel like a weirdo." Caio's voice now sounds more urgent. "You are not weird. You are incredible."

Don't fall in love with someone who doesn't make you feel beautiful, my mom said this morning. I still don't feel *beautiful* when I'm with Caio. But in this moment, I feel incredible. And it's a really great feeling.

"No need to apologize anymore. For anything," he finally says, resting his head on my arm.

He then grabs my hand, brings it to his lips, and gives it a little kiss. I think it's the most intimate gesture I've ever experienced. Even more than his fingers in my hair. Even more than his tongue in my mouth.

"Good night," I say in the lowest of whispers. But I'm sure he heard it, because we are so close to each other. *Really, really close.*

DAY 14

I WAKE UP TO CAIO whispering things that, unfortunately, are not pledges of eternal love.

"Yes, Mom. I miss you, too," he says in a low voice into his phone, still lying by my side. "Everything's fine here. I'll see you tomorrow. Give Dad a hug for me. Bye."

He hangs up, comes closer to me, and kisses my cheek. I want to kiss his mouth, but I have a feeling that I might have awful morning breath.

"Imagine your mom's face if she found out that this is what you do when you hang up the phone," I say, pointing at my cheek where he just planted a kiss.

"She would go ballistic." Though he laughs when he says it, there's concern in his eyes. "But you know, even with all of her eccentricities, I miss her."

"They'll be here tomorrow. That's just around the corner," I say with a lump in my throat. "Where are they, again?"

"In Chile, celebrating their anniversary," he says. "They spent the last couple of days visiting some islands full of penguins. My parents are obsessed with penguins, actually."

I let out a confused laugh.

"Long story short, penguins are faithful," Caio explains. "They stick with their partners forever. And if one of them dies, the other one stays alone for the rest of its life. Believe it or not, my parents find that to be romantic."

"Oh, come on! It's kind of cute."

"Yes, very cute. This idea of living the rest of your life by yourself, haunted by your dead penguin husband because you simply cannot move on with life."

"You're a monster, Caio."

"I just don't think that's how love works. It's too dramatic, this whole 'I will love you forever, even after you die, and I will never love anyone else because my heart is forever yours,' you know?"

"My favorite couple is Elizabeth and Mr. Darcy from *Pride and Prejudice*," I respond. "And they spend ninety percent of the book basically hating each other. So I think I like me some drama."

"My favorite couple is us," Caio says with a smile, and I almost have a breakdown because I most definitely DIDN'T SEE THAT ONE COMING.

"Caiolipe?" I suggest our couple name, because it's the smartest answer I can think of on the spot.

"Lipecaio?" he offers, laughing.

"Calipé is cool."

"That sounds like a car part."

"Better than Felicaio, though."

"Never mind all that," he says, stroking my face and kissing my lips, apparently not minding my morning breath.

*

My mom doesn't know how to behave in the presence of two people who have spent the night making out. She keeps winking or smiling at the two of us, and when it becomes humanly impossible to deal with this level of embarrassment, I decide it is time to invite Caio on a second date.

"We need to get out of here," I say, sounding urgent.

"Get out of here like grab all the money we have, hop on an interstate bus, and take an unforgettable road trip?" he answers, not showing much interest, still looking at his phone.

"Not a bad idea. But I was thinking of going to Dalva's Café."

His face lights up in a giant smile.

Dalva's Café is the closest thing to a Starbucks franchise in my town. But it has more Frappuccino options (including a surprisingly good guava flavor), and it's more affordable. The décor is cozy, full of old stuff (or *vintage*, as it were), with pleasant, soft lighting. I'm not a date connoisseur, but I think Dalva's is the perfect place for one.

"I want to eat their Belgian waffle until I get so sick I pass out," Caio says excitedly.

So romantic.

*

When we get there, the place is a little crowded, but we find ourselves a table in the back. The table is round and small, which makes our legs bump into each other all the time.

I'm far from complaining about that.

A nice server takes our orders, and we look at each other and enjoy thirty seconds of quiet before Caio starts laughing.

"It's funny to be here with you right now. Like this, you know?" He squeezes my hand briefly, then lets it go. "Just a few days ago, during one of those awkward silences between us, I'd text Becky asking for tips on what to say to start a conversation with you."

"At least you have Becky to reach out to. When *I* wanted to start a conversation with you, I had to google it!" I say, and he laughs.

"Seriously?"

"If you saw my search history, perhaps you wouldn't be sitting here with me today," I say, grabbing my phone from my pocket and showing him the screen, because I think it'll be funny.

I go to Google and tap the search bar, and right underneath, my last few searches show up:

"How to start a conversation without sounding awkward"

"Scented candles how to make"

"How many pajamas does a person need?"

"Do pajamas need to be washed every day?"

"Is Pisces and Cancer a good match?"

And right there, in the middle of all my questions, I read, "How do I know if I'm in love?" and block the screen immediately. But I think Caio saw it before I did.

He's looking at me with a calm smile, and I am a little ashamed. Because I was just trying to be funny, to show him the weird things that I look up when I'm bored. I wanted him to see I'm fun, not desperate.

I swallow hard and don't say anything. The server comes back with our orders, and I'm relieved to have something to occupy my mouth with.

"Did you figure it out?"

"If I have to wash my pajamas every day?" I ask, trying to change the subject, which makes him laugh.

"No need to be ashamed. It's just that . . . I wanted to know, too," he says, handing me his phone. On his screen, I can see his search history, and I'm amazed by the possibility of getting into his head for a few seconds:

"How to make brigadeiro without it sticking to the bottom of the pan"

"Animated musicals"

"Are Pisces romantic?"

"Are Pisces hard to get?"

"Harry Styles no shirt"

"First date tips"

"How to know if he's into you"

I take a deep breath, reading line by line, and then look at him with a relieved smile.

"I don't know what Google told you, but I can confirm that I am, in fact, into you," I say with a wink that probably makes me look creepy, because he starts laughing.

"Maybe it would have been easier to have asked you from the start, instead of hoping Google would give me all the answers," he says.

"When did it start?"

"What do you mean?"

"You said you could have asked me from the start. When was that? When did you stop and think that it was possible you were into me? And what did you see in me? Because honestly—"

"Lipé, stop," Caio interrupts me. "I don't remember the precise time. It probably started when I woke up and found out you'd left the book for me. Or the time you set aside a piece of cake for me and put the glass of milk close to my chair for breakfast. When you told me about your problems, and I realized that having a mom who accepts you is not the immediate solution to everything. When you listened to me crying and complaining about things that I have no idea how to solve. There was no beginning. It was all of those things that made me like you."

When I come back to myself, I realize my mouth is open and there's a piece of waffle in it that I simply forgot to chew while I was listening to Caio.

"That silly face also really helped," he says, placing his hand on my chin and closing my mouth. "What about you? When did you start to like me?"

I pause for a moment, trying to determine the best answer. I could say it was the day we played mermaids together, but I should probably save that story for when we exchange our wedding vows.

"It's been a long time, actually. It was before. Way before these last fourteen days."

"I'm glad you didn't wait any longer. Because I'm really scared of making a move. I'm a little—"

"Slow. Yeah. Becky told me," I say, smiling.

"So are you telling me that the two of you have talked about *this*?" he says, gesturing with his finger at the two of us.

"Actually, she was one of the people who made *this* happen," I say. "Have you already updated her on the rest of the story?"

"Just the basics, but she's desperate for more details. She

sent me about two hundred texts asking how the date went, if I'm happy, if *you're* happy."

"Let's send her a pic!" I suggest, not knowing where the idea came from.

I hate taking pictures. I hate the idea of having an image of me frozen for all eternity. I hate having to get ready for the photo, because I never know which face to make, so I always end up with a strange grimace, so I won't make my discomfort so obvious.

But I have no time to say all that because when I look up, Caio has already pulled his chair next to me and rested his head lightly on my shoulder. I look straight ahead, and the front camera of his phone is already on, and on-screen I see Caio, photogenic as ever, and me, clearly without a clue as to what I'm doing.

Caio doesn't wait for me to get ready. He starts to press the button, taking one selfie after another. I try to look brave, then nice, and then neutral. But all the photos end up being taken in between poses, and my face looks awful in all of them.

"Can you take it easy with that button?" I protest.

"Can you put a smile on your face? Because your smile is beautiful," Caio answers.

And, inescapably, I smile.

"Much better," he says between one photo and the other.

"You're not the first to say that. About my smile, I mean?" I say self-consciously.

"Who was the other guy?" Caio is so interested in my answer that he even lets go of the phone.

"Easy, easy. It was just my therapist." I laugh and take his hand.

And he doesn't let go.

And we stay there for some time, holding hands under the table while we pick the best photo to send to Becky.

Caio's head is on my shoulder, the air smells like fresh coffee and cake, and I could sit here for hours and hours. But in the following moment, when the front door of Dalva's Café flies open and three guys walk in boisterously, Caio moves away from me immediately.

He gets up quickly, puts his chair back in place, and stares at the ceiling, avoiding my eyes.

Caio asks for the check and doesn't let me pay for anything. ("You paid for the movies yesterday" is his argument). On the way out, we walk past the three guys, and one of them recognizes Caio. The three of them say a nice hello, and Caio answers hurriedly, then runs out of the café, his head hung low, not even checking to see if I'm following or not. He doesn't introduce me to the three guys.

When we get to the street, I ask if everything is okay, and Caio tries to change the subject.

"Yeah, nothing's wrong. I really just wanted to leave. I need to start packing, you know? Tomorrow, life goes back to normal."

The way he says all that gives my paranoid mind a lot of material to start working on.

*

Here's my conclusion: Caio knows those three guys from school. Classmates, probably. People he wouldn't mind meeting on the street at all if he hadn't been with me. If he hadn't been holding hands and leaning his head against my shoulder. If he wasn't dating a fat guy.

It's nothing new. Even I've thought something like that. When we come across a couple where one person is thin and the other one is fat, we tend to come up with a thousand explanations for that couple's existence, and none of them is "They must love each other."

"That guy must have a fetish."

"The fat dude must be rich."

"He was probably thin when they started dating, and now the thin guy would feel bad breaking up with him."

Whether they're a fetishist, gold digger, or coward, the thin one is always seen in a negative light. And that was probably what Caio was trying to get away from.

When we get home, Caio treats me like normal, as if nothing happened. Here, inside my apartment, there's a safety zone where he can kiss me, hug me, and sleep by my side without fear. But tomorrow, Caio will leave, and—he said so himself—life will go back to normal.

In the normal state of things, he's there, and I'm here. He's not my friend, much less my boyfriend. He'll go back to being the neighbor kid from apartment 57.

We eat dinner in silence, and my mom must notice something went wrong, because her winking has stopped for the time being.

And now, sitting on my bed while I watch him organize his oversized leopard-print suitcase, folding his clothes one by one and removing all his belongings from my bedroom, I feel like I have nothing left to lose.

"What is it going to be like after you leave?" I ask.

"What do you mean? The two of us?"

"Yes. Us."

"How do you want it to be after I leave?"

"For a start, I think it would be nice if you stopped answering my questions with more questions," I say, and my tone is much ruder than I intended it to be.

"Felipe, what's happening?"

"It's nothing." I give up on starting this discussion.

Caio stops folding his clothes, steps away from his suitcase, and sits in bed with me.

"Five minutes," he says, placing a hand on my knee.

"What are you talking about?"

"Let's play a game. We have five minutes to say anything that comes to our mind. No consequences. And if you don't want to discuss it after the five minutes are up, we pretend like nothing happened," Caio explains.

"You know that's the worst idea in the world, right? And that there are thousands of chances this won't end well?"

"It's better than standing here all quiet without saying what you really feel," Caio answers.

Oh, he wants feelings? I can give him that.

"Five minutes, then. I'll start." I position my phone between the two of us so I can check the time. "Oh, and one more rule. You can't answer questions with more questions. Deal?"

"Is this rule for the five minutes, or for life?" he asks.

This game is going to be a disaster.

When my phone's clock goes from 9:34 p.m. to 9:35 p.m., I start talking.

"I didn't like the way you walked out of the coffee shop today, running in front of me. I felt like you were ashamed of me. And then I felt ridiculous that I felt that way, since we don't have anything yet."

"I'm sorry, Lipé. I . . . I didn't want you to feel that way. It's just that—"

"I'm scared of what it's going to be like when you leave.

I have a long list of insecurities, and I wish I could stop feeling this way, always insecure. Sooner or later, you'll realize you can get someone way better." I keep talking. I'm like a machine gun full of feelings.

"I'm afraid, too," Caio says, raising his voice, and making it clear that he doesn't want to be interrupted.

9:36 p.m.

"My fear isn't about you, or the two of us," Caio starts. "The truth is, I'm not ready to come out of the closet. Not at school, and much less at home. I see people telling stories about how important that was to them, but I can't see how doing so could be a good thing for me. Coming out to my family would be the worst decision of all time. My mom isn't like yours. That's why I ran away at the coffee shop. Those three guys from school aren't mean to me. They're just my classmates, that's all. But if they saw me with you, word could get around. And I don't want you to think that I want to hide—or to hide you. I just don't feel . . . ready," he says all at once.

I feel the weight of his words on my shoulders. The weight of everyone being full of problems.

9:37 p.m.

"I'm not ready, either. For a bunch of stuff," I say, thinking back to last night. "I'm sorry that I thought what was happening was about me. It's hard to believe someone can really like you when you spend your entire life hearing that you're nothing but a disgusting fat guy."

"It's hard to believe you can really be happy with someone when you spend your entire life hearing that being gay is wrong and your fate is to burn in hell," Caio admits, his breathing irregular.

The sadness in his voice hits me hard.

"People are wrong. You can be happy," I say.

9:38 p.m.

"They're wrong about you, too. You are not disgusting."

I let a smirk escape, one that signifies, "Yeah, right." It's my automatic reaction. Caio stands up, and I'm led to believe he's given up on the five-minute game—that he's given up on me.

But he only walks to the other side of the room, rips Eddie's drawing of me in a Batman costume from the wall, and places it on my lap.

"Don't forget that there are people who see this when they look at you."

9:39 p.m.

I fall silent, looking at the drawing. I notice every stroke, every instance where the colored pencil went outside the lines . . . every detail of this image that makes me a superhero.

"I want to help you," I say. "If you feel afraid of being

who you really are. If you question your parents' love. If you doubt what you really can do. I want to help you go through it all. Please, lean on me."

"I already am. Even after the fifteen days are done. Even when I go back to apartment 57. I want to be with you. You are beautiful."

9:40 p.m.

The five minutes are up, and I don't know how to react. My mouth is hanging open, and Caio takes advantage of it and kisses me. A soft, sweet, delicate kiss this time.

"Believe me when I say . . ."

Another kiss.

"That you are amazing . . ."

And another.

"Your hair smells great . . ."

Another.

"And I like the little dimple at the end of your nose . . ."

A confused laugh.

And then another kiss.

"You are beautiful, Felipe. You really, truly are."

Suddenly, it seems like I've heard enough, because there are no more pauses between each kiss. We lie in bed, and I feel my body go hot.

When Caio puts his hands on my hips, my instincts tell me to shrink away and escape. But I don't do that. Because this time I don't feel ashamed. I don't feel like a disgusting fat guy who doesn't deserve to be touched.

I feel beautiful.

And when Caio touches me, there's no aversion in his touch. Unlike all the times I've been shoved, pinched, and teased, Caio's touch makes me feel good. When I lie on my side so he can hug me and fit his body into mine, I don't worry about whether my belly droops.

I feel a cold tingle when he runs his hand down my shirt, and I realize that I might not be totally ready. But I feel better when I notice that the lights are on, and he can see every detail of my skin. And I don't mind.

I feel comfortable here, and that's when I decide to enjoy his body, too. My hands, paralyzed on his shoulders up until now, slide down his arms. I caress his hips and start to discover every detail of his body, little by little. He notices how curious I am and lies still for a time, granting me permission to explore. Caio's skin is hot, and I feel his heavy breathing when I run my hand over his chest.

"You are beautiful, too," I say in a whisper.

And when he runs his hand along my face to give me another kiss, it occurs to me that if the word *beautiful* had a million different meanings . . .

Caio would be all of them.

DAY 15

LAST CHRISTMAS, MY MOM AND I went to the beach and stayed at a fancy hotel. I don't know much about hotels, but to me, if it has an all-you-can-eat breakfast buffet, it's fancy.

I have a vivid memory of a nap I took at that hotel. More specifically, I remember a dream in which a phone kept ringing and ringing, and when I finally picked up, no one answered. And it just kept on ringing forever. I tried ripping out the cord, throwing the receiver against the wall, but it simply wouldn't stop.

That dream could probably be a wonderful metaphor about how I deal with my problems in real life, but in the end, it was just the hotel room phone that was *actually* ringing, and the noise invaded my sleep.

Today the same thing happened. But it's not a phone that's blaring.

"Caio!"

I hear a voice screaming, and in my heavy sleep, it takes me some time to determine if the voice is coming from inside my head or the real world.

"Caio!" the voice bellows again, louder this time.

Despite how loud the shouting is, what really wakes me up are steps in the hallway. Don't ask me how, but in a split second I know exactly what I need to do.

I take one look at Caio sleeping by my side (beautifully, by the way), apologize in a whisper, and push him out of the bed. He falls onto the mattress on the floor, the loud voice yells, "Caio!" one more time, and he wakes up with a fright.

It all happens too quickly. Caio looks at me, one eye open, the other closed; looks at the door, still locked from the night before; and looks at me again, a little more nervous this time.

He gets on his feet, stumbles on something, and turns the lock, and when the door opens, there she is. Sandra, Caio's mom. The woman with the shrill voice. My (I've always wanted to say this) mother-in-law.

My hair is messy, my face is all wrinkled, and the shorts of my pajamas show too much of my legs. But Sandra doesn't mind, because in the blink of an eye, she's already covering Caio with kisses. Many, many kisses.

"I missed you so much." *Kiss*. "Your dad, too, but I missed you more." *Kiss*. "We took so many pictures!" *Kiss*. "And we have something for you." *Kiss*. "But it's a surprise."

The reunion lasts a few minutes, and I just sit there watching, half-embarrassed, half-happy.

Caio's mom is different from mine in several aspects. She's

shorter, her hair is really dark (almost blue), and it probably takes a lot of time and dedication to make it look as good as it does. The way she's neatly dressed and the way her makeup is flawless seem almost impossible for someone who just landed on a plane from Chile.

But above all else, she's affectionate. In an exaggerated, loud way, perhaps. But one could never question that she loves Caio more than anything in the world. And in the end, that makes me smile.

"Are you all packed? Shall we go home?" she asks.

"Yes, all packed," Caio says, pointing to the suitcase in the corner of the bedroom.

And that's when she notices me.

"Hi, Felipe, good morning! I'm sorry if I woke you." She smiles. "How was the break? Did you two have a fun time together?"

You have no idea, Sandra is what I think.

*

From all the goodbyes in the house, it almost seems as though Caio is off to Hogwarts, not to the fifth floor of the building. I bring his suitcase to the living room because it's the most affectionate thing I can do with his mom right there. The smell of coffee has taken over the apartment, and my mom tries unsuccessfully to organize the kitchen table so she can entertain our guests.

"Can I get you a coffee, Sandra?" my mom offers, grabbing a piece of clay and hiding it in the freezer.

"I can't stay long, honey," she says. "Mauro is coming upstairs with our suitcases. I just stopped by for a moment to get Caio."

"Just a little cup. To relax after your trip," my mom insists, as if it were a good idea to put caffeine in the body of a woman who just got home at seven in the morning, screaming her lungs out.

"I'm not about to say no to someone who looked after my child for two weeks, am I?" Sandra answers, sitting at the table and seeming uncomfortable when she catches a glimpse of the pair of breasts on one of the canvases my mom is painting.

I don't know if this is normal for everyone, but I have the power to decipher my mother's looks. All I need is one glance from her and I can tell if she's happy, anxious, or annoyed at something I did. The look my mom gives me right now means, "Go into the living room. I need a moment alone with this woman."

I nod to Caio (since he doesn't have the power of deciphering my mom's looks), and the two of us head into the living room together. We sit on the small couch, and he touches my leg with his.

"I miss you already," he says softly, staring at the floor.

"Don't be so dramatic, Caio," I answer, and give his knee a little squeeze.

We go silent, trying to hear what our moms are saying. It's not a very difficult task; it's not like I live in a mansion. The kitchen is right there, and Caio's mom is a loud talker. It's almost as if we never left.

"Again, Rita. Thank you so much for having my son over. Mauro insisted I should leave him by himself, but you're a mother, too. You know I would never forgive myself if something happened to him while I was far away," Sandra explains.

"It wasn't a problem. He was no trouble at all. Caio is a very good kid," my mom says.

"Ah, I have no doubt about that," Sandra says, full of pride. "The problem is bad influences, you know what I mean? One invite to a party here, then he starts spending the night over there. And then drinking, drugs . . ."

Caio laughs quietly, and I can visualize my mom doing her best not to roll her eyes.

"Caio seems to be surrounded by wonderful people. Friends that he loves very much," my mom says, voice firm.

"I know. Mauro and I love our son more than anything in the world. But we can't watch our children all the time, can we? And sometimes that's scary, isn't it?"

"Look, Sandra, I only had Caio over here for fifteen days. But it was enough to get to know how amazing he is. You must be very proud to have a son like him," my mom responds, her voice a little louder now.

"I am. I couldn't be prouder."

And Caio's face opens up in a smile, and he squeezes my hand.

"I told you so," I whisper so only he can hear.

☀

I spend the whole day looking for things to do. Things to distract me from how different the house looks now that Caio isn't around. Ultimately, I decide to start putting my vacation plans into action. The ones I had before Caio showed up.

I catch up with my TV shows, bingeing several episodes nonstop. I organize my books and designate a few for donation. I get lost in absurd thoughts about what the future holds, coming up with theories that make me anxious and desperate. The usual.

I feel like telling Caio everything about my day, even though I know nothing extraordinary has happened. But when I pick up my phone to text him, I realize I don't have his number. After fifteen days. After some (several) kisses. After this whole story. I don't even have the guy's number.

Of course, that's not a problem, because the internet is a thing. I go to each one of his social media accounts, which for a long time I used to browse like a creepy stalker, and finally add Caio. One at a time, I click all the follow and add buttons, until he becomes a part of my online life as well.

Now all I need to do is wait until he follows me back.

And the anticipation is killing me.

I stare anxiously at my phone screen every time it buzzes (and also when it doesn't), but it's never anything from Caio. It's always a notification from a game I don't play anymore, some email with a promotion from an online store, or my great-aunt Lourdes tagging me in a Facebook post, which, by the way, has happened twice in the last hour. My sixty-four-year-old great-aunt tagged me in *two* posts in the last sixty minutes (a photo with the caption "Have a blessed weekend" and a soufflé recipe with the caption "Show this to your mom xoxo"). And in that same period of time, Caio hasn't even had time to click accept on my friend request.

When my phone buzzes again and I've come to the conclusion that I need to block my great-aunt, I'm surprised by a text from an unknown number:

I got your number from Becky!

I stare at the phone screen like a goof, not knowing what to say. Which is nothing new.

I'm afraid I'll seem too needy, or too clingy, or too dramatic. Just to be sure, I send a reply that makes me sound like all three:

Now I'm the one who already misses you.

Caio:

And *I'm* the one who's dramatic.

Felipe:

How're things over there?

Caio:

Hard.

My parents just showed me photos from their trip.

All 1,245 of them.

I'm not joking.

There really are 1,245.

My dad connected the memory card to the TV.

And now there's kind of a penguin slideshow going on

Felipe:

So fun!!!!

Caio:

You're ridiculous ♥

Felipe:

And what was the surprise your mom had for you?

Caio replies with a selfie of him wearing a Chilean hat, with the little strings coming down his ears and tied together under his chin. He is the cutest thing ever to inhabit the received folder in my phone.

Caio:

This was the surprise.

A hat!!!

Felipe:

You look so good in it. But I'm a little disappointed in your mom because I expected it would at least be a penguin hat! 😊

Caio:

There are more than enough penguins in this house already.

And then he sends me a photo of a fridge with a huge collection of stuffed penguins on top. I didn't even know it was possible to put so many penguins on top of one single refrigerator. There's an additional shelf above the main collection that holds another collection of smaller penguins. And the fridge door is covered in penguin magnets. It's a little creepy, to be honest.

Caio:

I present to you:

My fridge!!!!

Hahahaha

Felipe:

Very modern.

Caio:

That's my family.

Sorry!!!

But you have to accept it!

Felipe:

I'll accept them. I might have a hard time accepting you pressing enter all the time instead of keeping it all in one single message, though.

Caio:

RIDICU

LOUS

!!!!

The day goes by as Caio and I text. The sad feeling of having said goodbye fades a bit every time I remember that he's literally only an elevator ride away. I feel like getting into said elevator and inviting him to go to the supermarket with me, take a walk around the square, or anything, really. Just so we can be together for a little while longer. I think this is the answer Google couldn't provide when I asked how to tell if I was in love.

By the time night comes, I'm already tired. I woke up early to Sandra's screams and didn't sleep at all after that. I get ready for bed after dinner, and without Caio's mattress on the floor anymore, my room seems huge.

I lie in bed, text Caio good night, and melt every time he sends me the kissing face emoji. It's not the normal kiss emoji; it's the kiss emoji *with a heart*.

Lying down and staring at the ceiling, I fixate on the star that glows in the dark. I think back to the first time I noticed it, the first night that Caio slept in my room.

I wish he would like me.

That was my wish to the star. I thought about wishing for him to fall in love with me, but I wasn't sure if that would work, since I didn't know how the wish-upon-a-glow-in-the-dark-star thing worked, or if it was anything like Aladdin's genie, who can't make people fall in love.

So I figured that if he at least *liked* me, that would be enough.

And in the end, my wish came true. I don't know if we'll love each other forever, like penguins do. But I know he likes me. And I like him. I always have, in fact. But it feels different now, ever since I opened up and let myself be liked back.

In the last fifteen days, I've learned a lot, and now it all plays out like a movie in my head. I've always enjoyed my alone time. Being my own company has never been a problem for me, and on the day Caio arrived, I was freaked out by the possibility of him ruining my solitary vacation.

But in all that time I spent by myself, I never really thought about the things that make me happy. I guess I've always been so busy trying to avoid being unhappy that I never found a way to be happy.

As I consider all of this, I feel like I'm close to uncovering some big revelation about myself—the kind of thing I'll share in therapy that'll make Olivia smile and be proud of me.

Maybe it will even help me find out where my sudden bravery came from and solve this week's challenge before my deadline. And then, so I don't end up forgetting everything, I decide to write it down.

I think again about creating a blog for profound and enlightened texts in the future (I hope it will work out this time), but at the moment, the notepad on my phone is enough. My head is still a little confused, so I decide to make a list. I can organize my ideas better that way. I grab my phone and start typing.

15 things I like but didn't know I liked until 15 days ago:

1. I like talking. Not texting or over the phone. I like talking and being heard. Giving my opinion and listening to others' points of view.

2. I like the color red. I always thought gray and black were the only colors I could wear. But red looks good on me.

3. I like sleeping in pajamas. It's way better than sleeping in old clothes, because pajamas are clothes that just stand there the whole day, waiting for you to sleep in them. Pajamas are more loyal than old clothes.

4. I like kids, because they can see a hero where no one else would.

5. I like Musical Wednesdays. (Yes, Mom, if you're reading this, it's true; you win.) I've always thought the idea was a bit silly, but honestly, how can one not like an official day of the week when you and your mother sit down to watch a movie where people sing the entire time? If I ever have kids (or kittens), we will have Musical Wednesdays forever!

6. I like the relief that comes with getting things all out in the open—even if it's a swear word—and not taking bullying. It's a hundred times better than just keeping my head down.

7. I like being surrounded by friends. I always thought that being in the middle of a group of people was the worst place to be, but I discovered that it feels completely different when you *want to* be with them.

8. I like coffee, even when I'm not hungover. But it needs sugar (at least three spoonfuls).

9. I like going to the library, because it reminds me of my grandma in a good way (and the smell of books is a bonus).

10. I like lying in my mom's bed to talk, because it feels like the world goes back to being simple.

11. I like holding hands at the movies, because having someone's hand to gently squeeze makes the movie more exciting. Even if it's a never-ending and senseless fight between robot zombies and humankind.

12. I like it when my hand is kissed; it's the most wonderful sensation of them all.

13. I like kissing. A lot. For real, kissing is really great. I want to kiss every day, if possible.

14. I like being touched when I feel like being touched. I've always treated my body like a grenade that's about to explode, as if no one ever wanted to come close to me, and even if they did, it would be best not to touch me. But my body is not a bomb.

It takes me some time to come up with the last item on the list. I lie there and wait for it to reveal itself miraculously, but it doesn't. What does appear is a text that surprises me.

Caio:

Meet me at the elevator.

Felipe:

Now? Have you lost your mind?

Caio:

It has to be now!

It'll be fun.

Trust me!

Felipe:

Caio, it's almost midnight.

Caio:

Meet me at the elevatooooorrrr!!!!!

Felipe:

Calm down, I'm coming. I was just playing hard to get.

And I do. I leave the apartment wearing my now-famous Batman pajamas (which, in case you were wondering, have been washed and smell really good) and wait for the elevator in the building's cold hallway.

When the door opens, there is Caio, also in his pajamas.

The first thing he does is smile at me. The second is hug me. The third is give me a quick kiss, not minding the security camera.

"What are we doing here?" I whisper, not knowing why I'm whispering.

"I wanted to see you. And I had a wild idea," he answers with a sly smile.

"Caio, if you're thinking of eloping like a couple madly in love, it's not gonna happen. Because I have no money and I'm not wearing the right clothes to run away together."

Caio laughs loudly, and the sound makes me feel good.

"We're not even leaving the complex. Don't worry. But be careful. We're about to do something illegal," he says mysteriously.

"From zero to a hundred, what are the chances that I'll wake up in jail tomorrow?"

"Zero."

"Then let's do it," I say as the elevator door whirs open.

*

POOL HOURS

8 A.M. TO 7 P.M.

That's what the sign above the entrance to our pool says. I'm not sure how I got here. Caio was pulling me gently by the arm, we walked right past the nearly sleeping doorman, and here we are. By the pool, on a cold, full-moon night, and I have no idea what's going on.

"I have no idea what's going on," I clarify.

"Me, neither. But I suddenly wanted to come here. Our vacation is almost over, my parents are back from their trip, and I really wanted to see you. I thought it would be a good idea to come here and talk. It's out of sight. No one would come here so late at night," he says with a glint in his eye.

"Aaaah, now I see what you want," I say, inching closer for a kiss. His kiss is calm, passionate, and tasting of toothpaste. I think this might be the best one so far.

Caio grabs me by the hand, sits by the pool with his feet in the water, and signals for me to sit next to him. And I do, because there's no other place I'd rather be right now.

"My mom noticed there was something different about me," Caio says, leaning his head against my shoulder.

"What do you mean? Is she suspicious or something? Does she know about us? Did she ask you a bunch of questions like I'm doing right now?" I say a little hastily.

"No, nothing like that. She just told me I seemed . . . happier. I had no idea it was that obvious."

"There are some kinds of happiness that are as obvious as a neon sign blinking over your head."

"My neon sign must have your name on it," Caio says, and we drift into a comfortable silence.

But I decide to break it.

"It was on the day we played mermaids," I say.

"What?"

"Remember when you asked me when I started liking you? It was on that day. We were kids, and I asked if you wanted to play mermaids, and—"

"And we swam with our legs crossed until the sky went dark," Caio finishes my sentence. "I remember that day."

"It was a good one." I hug Caio's side and squeeze him against my body.

Then Caio wriggles out of my hug, stands up, takes off his shirt, and looks at me.

"Want to play mermaids?" he says, a silly smile on his face.

And then he dives in, splashing water all over me.

I sit there, watching Caio swim from one side of the pool to the other, apparently comfortable, as if the night weren't cold, and the water even colder.

"Hey! Come swim with me!" he calls to me.

My legs shake when I get up, and I don't know if it's because they went numb from the cold water or if it's because of the decision I'm about to make. I look around, feeling as if I'm being watched, while Caio continues to swim and call my name.

Out here, under the bright moon, there's no way to turn off the lights. No way to close the door and cover the windows. Out here, he can see me the way I am. And I can't believe what I'm about to do, but without second-guessing it, I take off my shirt and dive into the pool.

I spend a few seconds underwater, getting used to the temperature, and when I resurface to breathe, Caio is already floating by my side.

"You're cheating, that's not how you play mermaids," he says, pointing at my feet. "You have to cross your legs, and you're not allowed to touch the bottom of the pool."

I laugh. "Who came up with those rules?"

"The mermaids themselves. I'm just communicating for them," he says, placing his hand on my back to help me float, too.

When I start floating, Caio gives me another kiss (this time it tastes like chlorine), and I lose my balance. I float, then fall back underwater, and laugh—not minding that the moonlight shows each and every one of my imperfections, and that the water makes me appear twice my size.

"It's so good to be here with you," I say, hugging Caio and feeling him float in my arms.

"I think anywhere is good if I'm with you," he answers, kissing my neck (which, by the way, has just won the spot for favorite place to be kissed).

"Anywhere except a movie theater where they're playing the third *Zombie Robots*. We're not sitting through that again. I'm warning you ahead of time," I protest.

"I saw in a documentary once that the average person watches about one hundred and fifty very bad movies in their lives. This was our first. There are still a lot ahead of us," he says.

"Caio, that data makes no sense," I answer, and my chin starts shivering.

"I just wanted to be cute, leave me alone!" he says, play-fully splashing water on my face.

I turn around to dodge the splash, and Caio wraps his arms around my neck to try and steal a kiss. And then it comes to me—the final item on my list. It's not as revealing as I thought it would be, but I make a mental note so I won't forget:

15. I like the pool. For a long time, I pretended I didn't, because I was ashamed of my body. But tonight, floating next to Caio and looking up at the moon above us, I understand what makes me happy when I'm in the water. When I'm here, I feel weightless.

ACHNOWLEDGMENTS

Rafael, writing this book was an incredible journey that would have been way harder without you by my side. Thank you for listening to my drama on nights when everything I wrote felt like one big disaster, for encouraging me and giving me the best ideas, and for always being the first one to listen to a chapter as soon as I was done writing it. Even when it was late and all you wanted was to go to bed or play Pokémon or something. I love you.

Mirian, you are the only mom I have. So all the moms in this book have a little bit of you in them. Thank you for the inspiration that I'm going to carry for the rest of my life, for your unending love and care, and for trying to understand me even on the hardest of days. To my sister, my beautiful nephews, and all my family: You are always on my mind and in my heart. I carry you everywhere, and I hope to one day fill you with pride.

Tassi, when we first met, you told me that the agent's job is to let the writer write and take care of everything else. You took this statement to a whole new level, taking care of my career, my characters, and my personal crises, showing me every day how good it feels to work with a pro! Thank you for helping me to take Felipe's story to places I've never been.

To Lucas Rocha for sharing this amazing experience of being a Brazilian YA author published in the US for the first time. We've celebrated and cried and drank together so many times that it's hard for me to remember a time in my life when you were not around. Thank you for being such a great friend!

Mayra, thank you for being a loyal and patient friend, who endured me talking endlessly about Felipe's story from the very beginning, and for listening (literally, over our afternoon coffees where I'd read you the new chapters) to each piece of this story with such enthusiasm. Hearing you laugh as I read made me even more excited to keep going.

To all my friends, for all the love. Thereza, Fogs, Vito, Vinnie, André, Duds, and Davi. Thank you for reading this story and for helping me with the list of possible names for Felipe and Caio's cat. This story has a little piece of you in it.

Gabi, you were a huge help in writing the story of my life, standing by my side when no one else would. Thank you for being the Becky to my Caio.

Rainbow, thank you for all your support and inspiration. Your books make me feel lucky to be alive right now.

To the Alt team, my Brazilian publisher, you are all wonderful! Veronica, thank you for always believing in my stories and being an editor and a friend at the same time. Sarah, thank you for listening to all my insecurities during the writing process and for always sending me the best replies, such as "Hi, Vitor! The lack of commas in your email made me a little dizzy, but it was perfect to help me understand the drama," which I PRINTED AND HUNG ON MY WALL (seriously).

Thank you to the Scholastic team for treating my story with so much care and enthusiasm. To my editor, Orlando, for making this possible and for all your kind words and fun tweets; to the untenable concept of fate for putting my book in Orlando's hands at the right time; and to David Levithan, Baily Crawford, and Josh Berlowitz.

A huge thank you to translator extraordinaire, Larissa Helena, who captured Felipe's voice perfectly in a new language, and especially for coming up with "asspecialist." We couldn't have done it without you!

And, finally, thanks to all the people who fought and are still fighting for the rights of the LGBTQIA+ community. If today I get to publish a book about two boys who fall in love, I owe it all to you. Thank you for never giving up. We're in this fight together. The whole world is ours.

ABOUT THE AUTHOR

Vitor Martins lives in São Paulo, Brazil, and works as an illustrator and book marketer. He believes that representation in young adult literature is a powerful weapon, and his main goal as a writer is to tell stories of people who have never seen themselves in a book. Follow him online at vitormartins.blog and on Twitter and Instagram at @vitormrtns.